To Love, From Zion

HARREAM PURDIE

DEDICATION

I dedicate this book to my mother, Stephanie Major, who gave me life. To my late grandmother, Helen Major, who gave me unconditional love. To Helena, Ameen, Ameena, Haneefah, Sheaunna, and Lloyd, who gave me stories and for being on these journeys with me.

To Lynne Johnson, Elmore Johnson, Kendall McArthur and Annette Sample for being so caring and supportive of me. And to all of the teachers who encouraged me to read more and to write more.

To Love, from Zion

I conceive of my own life as a journey toward something I do not understand, which in the going toward, makes me better. I conceive of God, in fact, as a means of liberation and not a means to control others. Love does not begin and end the way we seem to think it does. Love is a battle, love is a war; love is a growing up.

James Baldwin

Nobody Knows My Name

_____

To Love, from Zion

To Love, From Zion

CONTENTS

To Love, from Zion

To Love, from Zion

ONE
DARE

"**I dare you to knock his books** out of his hands," my best friend Scooter whispered.

"Ok, bet." I said with a grin.

Despite my classmate Robert's clenched fist and stare, I smiled at him. Fully accepting Scooter's challenge, I knocked all of Robert's books to the floor. Robert let the books scatter to the floor. Then he took the first swing at my face hitting me square on the jaw. Fully anticipating Robert's reaction, I dropped my notebooks and pencil. I immediately fired back using the techniques I had learned from boxing at the neighborhood Rec center.

"Whoa," Scooter shouted.

I aimed for Robert's nose and eyes successfully landing three jabs. Scooter grabbed me and used his body to prevent us from going into a full out brawl.

With Scooter between Robert and me, I backed away laughing at how easily a fight could break out. Our commotion had caused a scene but not enough for us to get caught fighting. Robert retreated to his corner of the hall and I stopped resisting Scooter's hold. We laughed to keep our appearance low. But we knew sooner or later someone would tell.

Discretely, we sauntered to line up outside of Ms. Sample's Language Arts class. This was a typical day for a seventh grader at Roberts Vaux Middle School. This was how we entertained one another. Scooter and I would play this game called dare. One of us would dare the other to do something funny, risky, or violent, the more entertaining and hilarious the better. Then the other would have to comply. These games often ended with someone getting into trouble. For now, we seem to be in the clear.

We rushed to our seats as swiftly as we could. To keep from being caught, we pretended to give Ms. Sample our undivided attention. Ms. Sample began her lesson. Today, we are reading about Malcolm X. Ms. Sample is our favorite teacher, so we try to keep the disruptions to a minimal. But I can't prevent myself from laughing at Scooter's dare. I actually like Robert, his brother Shawn and I are good friends. But I couldn't lose a dare. Even though I would never dare Scooter to do such a thing.

Ms. Sample goes into the hook of her lesson. I'm a huge fan of Black History. But this was more than a black history lesson. Ms. Sample always chose interesting readings that provided life lessons. We were learning how Malcolm X decided to copy the dictionary in an effort to educate himself. Then suddenly, she gets a call on the classroom telephone. She answers and looks directly at me. "Darn," I thought.

"Robert" she paused. "And Zion Major, please report to Mrs. Lewis's office." Ms. Sample returned to her desk to write us a pass to the assistant principal's office. We were caught or maybe someone told, I thought. I took the pass. Then Robert and I walked to Mrs. Lewis's office.

As we walked, I thought to myself, not again. If I get in trouble today, how do I explain this to grandma? I cannot continue to get into trouble. I cannot continue to get pink slips. I don't want to follow in my older siblings' footsteps. But then I also thought, she has no proof that we were fighting. I'll deny it. Or better yet, I'll apologize to Robert now and let him know it was only a dare gone too far.

"You know I was just playing around" I said. "Robert, are we good?"

He turned to face me. "Zion, you play too much," he replied. "Way, way too much. But we're good. Just don't let it happen again."

"Cool." I calmly nodded. In that moment, the two of us had an unspoken pact not to rat the other out. Then we waited for Mrs. Lewis to speak with us individually. She first spoke with Robert. Then she addressed us both.

"If I could prove that you two were fighting, I would certainly suspend you both." Mrs. Lewis said. Then she let Robert go with just a warning.

"Did you intimidate that boy?" She asked. "He said that nothing happened. But I've talked with two other students who both claimed to have seen you hitting Robert. Is that true Zion?"

I couldn't believe she was asking me this. "I didn't threaten him," I said. "He's his own person. Nothing happened."

Mrs. Lewis shook her head at me. "Well I hope not. This is school Zion, you're here to learn not act out and cause trouble."

"I understand," I said. "But like he said nothing happened."

"Your mother would not be proud to hear about you misbehaving," she added.

I sucked my teeth and mumbled "I don't live with my mom."

"Sorry," she corrected herself. "I don't think your grandma would be happy to hear that you're acting up."

Her lecture only made me more frustrated and my mind began to block her out. Although Mrs. Lewis continued to talk, I completely tuned her out. There were too many things on my mind and this conversation only aggravated me more.

Mrs. Lewis recognized my frustration, but she couldn't quite place why I was acting out this time. She continued lecturing me, but I defiantly stared at the floor.

I stood still as tears welled in my eyes but never fell. I was too tough to show weakness. So I kept quiet.

"I want you to meet with Mr. El" she said. "Do you like chess? I think you would be good on the chess team."

"Okay," I murmured indifferently.

"I know you're angry, and I think this program could help," she added. And then she dismissed me to class.

Throughout the day, I pondered the possibility of the chess program. I knew Mr. El because all of the students talked about how cool and down-to-Earth he is. We also liked that he was funny but also professional. And we admired the fact that he was one of the few black male teachers at our school. Yet although we admired Mr. El, many of my friends viewed chess as a nerd's game.

In the past, I had been in more programs than you could imagine trying to deal with my anger problems. From counseling sessions to Boy Scouts, nothing was actually working. I still felt the need to be a rebel. And more importantly I wanted to win the approval of my peers.

So I tried out for the basketball team, but Mr. Edwards found that I lacked the necessary skills to play for the team. He advised me to play for the school's intramural program. And I listened.

At least Mr. El welcomes all students to chess club, I thought to myself. My strategy was to go so that I could learn the basics and begin building a relationship with Mr. El. If he knows my name and my face, maybe he could save me from getting into trouble in the future. Maybe he could also speak to Mrs. Lewis on my behalf.

I knew Mr. El was very serious about the Vaux Chess club. I did not want to subject myself to being teased for being smart and for being on the chess team. Even though the Vaux Chess club is a terrific team with an outstanding reputation, I'd rather play basketball and write raps. All of my friends respect basketball players and rappers. So for now, I'll agree to meet Mr. El just so I can save myself from being on Mrs. Lewis' bad side. I know she still believes in me.

◆ ◆ ◆ ◆ ◆

TWO

CHESS LESSON

Scooter and I walked home together as we did every day. We talked about our dares and how sometimes they go too far. Then I told him that Mrs. Lewis suggested I go to chess.

"Yo, Zion you should come," Scooter said excitedly.

Scotter was already a member of the chess team. He explained to me that in order to make the team, I had to prove that I was committed enough to learn the game and attend practices regularly. Practices were open to all students.

So I decided to give chess a try. I attended practice early in the morning. Mr. El enthusiastically welcomed all students to learn the game of chess. But he made it clear that he only wanted the best and most committed students to represent the team

He taught us that chess is more than just a board game. It requires strategic skill. On that first morning, I remember learning the board, the pieces, and their particular moves. We also learned that each player begins the game with sixteen pieces that are moved and used to capture opposing pieces.

"In chess, there are precise rules," Mr. El said. "The object is to put the opponent's king under a direct attack from which escape is impossible. This is called a checkmate."

Mr. El was a good teacher and an excellent coach. He knew how to motivate students who were interested in chess. "I can guarantee that chess will help you become a better student," he promised.

I wondered how chess would help me become a better student. I felt comfortable at the chess practices. I continued to go for about a week.

I became excited when Mr. El began teaching us strategies on how to checkmate an opponent in three to four moves.

When we got to Ms. Sample's class, I wanted to tell Scooter how well morning chess practice had been for me. While Ms. Sample explained the different sentence types, I leaned forward and tapped Scooter's shoulder. Trying to remain on task, Scooter turned his ear in my direction.

"What's up," he whispered.

"I think I like Chess, bro." I said. "I think I'm ready to play you."

"No you're ready to lose to me," Scooter corrected me. We laughed.

"Shhh," Ashley shushed us. "Ms. Sample'll hear you."

Ms. Sample sighed with relief when she turned to face the class. "Great job students. Now I need for you to read and analyze ten sentences. Circle the predicates and underline the subjects. Draw a line separating the clauses in the sentence. Then write the sentence type on the line." Ms. Sample paused to give us time to process her instructions. "Now turn to your partner and repeat the directions as they are printed on your assignment."

We did as instructed and in unison we read the directions aloud. "You may begin," Ms. Sample said.

The majority of the class immediately dived into their assignments. I attempted the first three sentences and stopped at the fourth. I wanted to tell Ms. Sample about chess, but I needed a legitimate reason to get her attention. I raised my hand.

As I hoped, Ms. Sample quietly came to assist me with my classwork. "Yes, Zion." She said, directing her attention to the papers on my desk.

"For number four, I'm not sure where the clause ends," I said. "I understand the predicate and the subject, but I'm confused about the clauses."

Ms. Sample took her time explaining to me the sentence and showed me how to recognize the clause and identify the sentence type. I valued her patience as a teacher. I wanted to tell her about chess practice and how much I enjoyed it.

"I started attending chess practice, Ms. Sample. And I think I want to try out for the team." I said.

"That's beautiful Zion," Ms. Sample said with a smile. "Well you know chess is a thinking man's game. It's not about winning it's about learning."

I didn't know what that meant, but I smiled and nodded. It felt good to know that by learning chess, I made Ms. Sample proud. But my pride was short lived. Almost immediately after Ms. Sample walked away to check on other students, insults were thrown at me.

"You're weird, Zion." Montez said.

"Takes one to know one," I said.

My response got the attention of my classmates. Their heads turned to face Montez. "I'm not the weirdo hype about chess," he said.

"But I bet I'd beat yo ass. You bastard!" I said taunting Montez.

My classmates gasped in shock at my response. I was proud of my witty remark. But Ms. Sample was not. She pulled a pink slip from her desk and immediately began writing. And again, I was getting into trouble. No matter how hard I attempted to travel the right path, negativity found a way to derail me.

◆ ◆ ◆ ◆ ◆

THREE

WRITE, ZION, WRITE

The consequence for using profanity in the classroom is a phone call home and a morning detention. I have already received six pink slips this school year, so I have exhausted my fair share of warnings. I got home to find grandma sitting at the dining room table with her arms folded across her chest. She was more than disappointed.

"A hard head makes a soft ass," grandma said. "Why are you so fixated on being the class clown?" Grandma gestured for me to come to her. She waved her hand at me. I frowned and walked closer to her. I knew Ms. Sample called to tell grandma about my misbehavior. Her disappointment was warranted. It's embarrassing to be told consistently about your grandson acting out in class.

When I got within arm's reach, she grabbed my shirt and pulled me in closer. With her other hand, grandma smacked me across my head. I cowered to protect my face. She hit me again on the back of my head. "Sit down right here," grandma said.

Grandma got up from her seat and pulled the chair from the table. I sat down. After two smacks at the head, I anticipated a few more hits from her. But grandma was done hitting and she was done fussing.

"You're going to write that teacher an apology letter," grandma said.

"Huh," I turned to grandma.

"You heard me clear, boy. You're going to apologize to your teacher."

I grabbed the pen and straightened the paper. Although I was embarrassed and ashamed to be hit, I knew grandma was right. I needed to apologize to Ms. Sample. But I just sat there twiddling my pen and staring at the blank page.

"Write Zion, write," Grandma said. I began writing my letter.

Dear Ms. Sample,

I write to apologize for my classroom behavior today. I know I was disrespectful with my comments to my classmate. I talked with my grandmother today and she explained to my why classroom behavior is important to creating a successful learning environment. I also understand that proper behavior is expected throughout the entire school. And I am sorry. I know my comments were not directed at you, but to another student. But I apologize for disrupting your lesson with rude and inappropriate remarks. It will not happen again. I understand that learning is the most important thing in life, and that I must not take it for granted. Please accept this letter of apology.

Sincerely,

Zion Major

Grandma stood over me as I wrote my letter. When I finished, she read over it. Satisfied with my letter, grandma dismissed me from the dining room table.

The next morning, I missed chess practice to attend my morning detention. I knew I had to see Mr. El eventually so I decided to let him know

"I'm sorry Mr. El but I won't be able to come to chess anymore," I said.

"Why Zion? Mr. El asked. "What's going on?"

"Mmmm I dunno," I mumbled. I kept my eyes low to avoid eye contact.

"Okay. Well, Zion, you're welcomed to continue practicing with us. And if you're serious just know we are doing big things. As you know, we are going to the National Scholastic Chess Championship in Knoxville."

"I'm sorry. But I'm going to be late to my morning detention," I said. I said "I'm sorry," when what I really am is embarrassed and confused.

As I walked to Ms. Sample's room, I tried to convince myself that I made the right decision. I had my mind made up that I would quit participating in the chess program altogether; a decision I probably will regret later on.

Secretly, I think it hurt Ms. Sample to write me up. And I'm not mad at her for doing so, I'm more so disappointed that I let her down. I want to apologize, but I think detention is enough retribution for my misuse of language.

When a student serves morning detention, the teacher usually requires the student to clean up or organize files for her. Ms. Sample made me wipe the classroom desk with disinfectant. Then she told me I could do school work for the remaining time.

"May I write in my journal" I asked.

"Certainly Zion You may write Ms. Sample said. "I didn't know you wrote"

"Mmm hmm," I mumbled as I sat at my assigned desk. I reached into my backpack and pulled out my tattered composition notebook. I flipped through the pages searching for incomplete thoughts or the first blank page I could find. I read over my last entry. I was complaining about Montez and how I wanted to fight him for calling me a "weirdo." I drew a fist punching through a brick wall on one page. The next page, I drew a pawn chess piece facing a king chess piece. Then underneath the chess pieces I wrote, "fuck Montez." My anger is the reason I'm here serving this detention now. I found a blank space to write.

"No more pink slips. No more detentions. I have to change my ways. I have to do better." I tried my best to motivate myself through writing. Then I drew a cloud around my written affirmation. I drew another cloud around the first cloud.

Then I remembered my apology letter. I thought about when would be the best time to give Ms. Sample my letter. I figured I should wait until my detention was served. I pulled the letter out of my backpack. I folded it once. And then I folded it again.

Ms. Sample printed some documents. Then she grabbed a manila folder from her desk drawer. She placed the documents in the folder and placed them on the edge of her desk.

I continued to write. In my journal, I organized a list of players to form an intramural basketball team. Since deciding to quit chess, I figured joining an intramural basketball team would better suit me. I was fast enough and strong enough to play basketball. And basketball is widely accepted by all of my peers. My weakness is my ball handling and my jumpshot. So far my list includes, Shawn, Brian, Jamaal and Sam. I just need one more person to have at least six players. Intramural rules require at least six players for four on four full court basketball. The games only last twenty minutes and there are two games each day after school. I would ask Scooter, but he is already a member of the chess team, which interferes with intramural games.

Just as I was concluding my thoughts, the morning bell rang. Ms. Sample stood up at her desk and called my name. I walked to her desk.

"Yes, Ms. Sample," I said.

"I don't want you using the type of language in class. Only people with a limited vocabulary talk that way. I know your grandmother raised you better than that. Here take these."

Ms. Sample handed me the manila folder with the printed documents inside. I opened the folder.

"Here are some writing competitions I'd like for you to consider," she said. "Each competition is for middle school and high school students. Some even offer cash prizes or academic scholarships. Read over them and give it some consideration."

I glanced at the papers inside. One read Philadelphia Writing Project Scholastic Art and Writing Awards and the other was the School District of Philadelphia student Writing competition.

"Yes, ma'am," I said.

"Now go to your homeroom," she said. "Let me know if you have any questions for me later today when I see you in class."

"I will Ms. Sample," I said. "I like to write. And also, I wanted to give you this." I handed Ms. Sample the apology letter. She didn't open it or look at it. She was mid-thought so she finished what she had to say.

"I know you like to write Zion," she said. "And keep writing Zion. Write, Zion, write."

♦ ♦ ♦ ♦ ♦

FOUR

HOME

If you visit Philadelphia, this is what you will see. A beautiful zoo, museums, and a bell called Liberty. You may go for a walk or go to the park. You may even visit a public monument or the Masonic lodge near City Hall. But you won't come visit my school. And you probably won't see the conditions of our Rec center. You'll never witness how there's only two swings that work. And you probably won't see the graffiti covered see-saw or the wobbly merry go round. You won't visit the Chinese store or the Papi store on our street corners. And you won't get to experience the constantly increasing prices at the Shop-n-bag on Girard Avenue. You won't see our bad roads with its many potholes. You won't come visit the abandoned houses that are just as frequent as the dilapidated houses some folks call home. More specifically, you won't see narrow Newkirk Street, where I live. But Philadelphia is my home and Newkirk Street is where I live.

At home, people are constantly yelling and complaining. If it is not my grandma, then it is my Aunt Helena. If it's not my brother and sisters, then it's my cousins. If it's not about the filth and dirt, then it's about someone touching someone else's things. If it's not about money, then it is about food.

I don't see the purpose in yapping and complaining all of the time. It's only going to annoy and aggravate everyone around you.

This environment makes me anxious. We like to call it home. But it doesn't always feel like a home. And what is home, anyway?

Is home a place where families live and feel safe and secure? Our house on Newkirk Street is the only home I know. I know we have a big dysfunctional family. There are many cousins, sisters, and brothers, an aunt, boyfriends, and grandma. I don't feel safe here. People here are always stealing. People here are always coming and going. People here use this house to get themselves right or to transition through, because Grandma owns this home. So we hide what we love. We protect what's sacred.

Grandma owns this house and she makes sure she reminds everyone in it. Her daughters and their boyfriends have all called this home. Her nieces, Rhonda and Maxine have once called this home. Her nephew Jeffrey has once called this home. My memories of this home include the comings and goings of many people. I was never told why or how long people would stay here. I remember always sharing a room. I remember always sharing my space. This crowded living space we called home. Even today I share a room. As I sit here by the back room's window, the only way to cool myself down is to bury my head in a book.

In my mind, home is more like an understanding and less like a physical space. In the confusion of this crowded home, I actually feel alone. When I notice the comings and goings of relatives and family friends, I become more aware of what is lacking here—peace.

◆ ◆ ◆ ◆ ◆

FIVE

POWERFUL NAMES

My grandma began a family tradition when she named my mother, Savannah, and my aunt Helena. Both are named after locations. So in our family, babies are named after locations. And the more I think about it, even grandma's name, Helen, has its own significance. She is named after the daughter of Zeus and Leda, born from an egg. I remember learning in school that the Trojan War was caused by Helen. In the Odyssey, Helen was the beautiful wife of Menelaus. Grandma is the matriarch of our family. She is the breadwinner in our home.

My mother's name is Savannah; it means grassland without trees. It is also the name of a city in Georgia and a river close to the Atlantic Ocean. My aunt, Helena, is named after the capital of Montana. She also shares the name of Roman empress and mother of Constantine the Great. My grandma was very intentional about choosing such powerful names.

My mother Savannah is crowned in victory; nothing greater than being a Major. She's the powerful Leo, strong, fierce, bold, and courageous. Mother of five beautiful lives each graciously blessed with powerful names

She named her first son, Zaire, after the Congo River in central Africa. He's the loyal and trustworthy one, born on the Taurus-Gemini cusp. He is virtuous, physically and mentally strong.

She named her first daughter America, after the continents. She is also the loyal and trustworthy one. She was born an ambitious Capricorn, responsible and resourceful.

She named her third child, India, after the subcontinent in Asia. She is the devoted believer, the down-to-earth, independent, and persistent Taurus. Her fourth child, she named Sydney, the admirable one. She is emotional and self-absorbed. She, like our mother, is a powerful Leo, strong, fierce, bold, and courageous.

And my name is Zion. I am named after the hill of Jerusalem on which the city of David was built. I am Savannah's youngest child. Her gift to me means noble and exalted. I love my name. Many people call Africa, Zion. I was born a conscientious Aries. I am generous, independent, optimistic, and courageous.

Our names are powerful. They were carefully chosen for each of us. In our lives we must make manifest the power in our names. Our lives must reflect the authority of our names. That means we must choose to know the meanings of our names and the purpose of our lives.

◆ ◆ ◆ ◆ ◆

SIX

GOT YOU BEAT

In my house, we have to compete for everything. In my neighborhood, you have to compete to survive. In school, you have to protect yourself.

Just getting to and from school, one could expect for a fight to break out. In school, young people learn to be rebellious. Students learn more about getting into trouble than we do English, math, and social studies standards.

It's pressure to smoke. It's pressure to drink. It's pressure to fight. It's pressure to date. It's pressure to have sex. It's pressure to make trouble.

If growing up involves a loss of innocence, a huge part of me doesn't want to. I remember arguing and fighting with my brother Zaire and my cousin London. We would go back and forth.

I bet you that I can beat you in racing.
You ain't faster than me.
On your mark, get set . . . go!
Huh, huh, huh, see huh I told you.

Now let's play hide-and-seek
I bet you'll never find me.
And if we play tag, I'll never be it.
We could do anything you want us to do
and I'll bet that I'm better than you.

You see that gate over there?
I bet you I can beat you to the top.
I can jump over that big rock.
You'd probably fall like "flop."

You can be Superman, but I'm Kryptonite.
You can be Hulk Hogan, but I'm Andre the Giant.
You can be Yokozuna, but I'm Lex Luger.
You can be Magic Johnson, but I'm Michael Jordan.
You can be Charles Barkley, but I'm Shaquille "the Shaq"
You see I still got you. You want to go on?

No matter what you say or do.
I'm going to be better than you.
It's just me.
You'll be better than somebody some day
Just not me

These were beautiful times. If growing up involves a loss of innocence, a huge part of me doesn't want to. I'd like to put store my good memories in a bottle like moments in a time capsule. I'd bury the bottle some place safe, some place memorable.

◆ ◆ ◆ ◆ ◆

SEVEN
THIRTEEN TWENTY-FIVE

Grandma opened the squeaky door and pushed the light switch up. "It's time to get up, boy," she said. "I'm up, grandma," I mumbled as I removed the thin sheet covering my legs.

"Wake your sisters up too," she added.

"Yes, ma'am," I replied.

Just across the room were my two sisters, India and Sydney. Today the three of us shared this room. And every morning grandma made sure we were up and ready for school.

As I dragged my body upright, I wiped the sleep from my eyes. "It's time to get up yall," I said to my sisters. Just up stairs, I could hear grandma yelling at my brother Zaire to wake him up. Zaire was a hard sleeper, often times requiring several attempts to wake him up. In the other bed of that same room, my sister America was probably awake or waiting to be awakened by grandma's silvery voice. And this was our morning routine at 1325 North Newkirk Street.

1325 was a house of love. It wasn't a lovely home. It wasn't a beautiful home. It was a three-story row-home on a narrow one-way street in North Philadelphia. Not only were bricks missing in places, but also the house front was in deplorable condition. The red paint was old and chipping away. The white screen door had reached its limit and was barely hanging on.

For most of my childhood, I recall being without more often than actually being with. We had no running water for several months at a time. One winter, grandma couldn't afford to pay the water bill. We resorted to filling gallons of water from a sympathetic neighbor's kitchen sink. And when the Philadelphia winters were too cold, we wore layers and crowded our electric heaters.

Our living conditions were also tight. Our home was always full. Four bedrooms: grandma had the second floor front room, Aunt Helena had the third floor front room, and the remaining two rooms were shared by us five. My Aunt Helena even shared her room with her son, London, and her boyfriend. Often times we slept wherever we felt comfortable.

Grandma made sure we made it to school on time every day. We had no excuses because grandma worked at our elementary school and it was only a five-minute walk just around the corner. If grandma didn't say she loved us often, she sure enough showed us through her selfless sacrifices. Grandma only had two daughters, my mother Savannah and my aunt Helena. Her love was evident in the way she disciplined us, the way she fed us, the way she taught us. She understood that as children we had no control over our mother's decisions. She did not speak negatively about our mother, despite our mother's drug problems. She showed her love through strict expectations and used discipline to make sure we understood that in order to succeed we must work hard and not make excuses.

1325 was a house of love because grandma made it that way. Whether we had or had not, she made sure we were provided for. She was consistently there for us, even though none of us directly asked for it. Loving us was her number one priority. And for that, I am forever grateful.

For a long time, I felt like a mistake. I felt like my grandmother inherited her daughter's unwanted children. I remember the shame I felt at knowing my cousin London had his mother and his father.

Shame comes to mind when I reflect on my childhood. I have memories of my cousin London spending time with both his mother and his father. My aunt Helena was a caring mother. She not only showed London love, her affection extended to her two nephews and three nieces. She not only spent time with us, she also taught us things. I recall the painful feelings of not having my mother there to share similar experiences. Those early moments in my childhood truly shaped my consciousness and my understanding of the world. In retrospect, what I recall the most about Newkirk Street are deep feelings of shame.

I was embarrassed because I felt unwanted. Despite grandma's unwavering love and support, I still want my mother. And for a long time, I wanted my father. I reminisce envying my cousin London. My Aunt Helena taught us how to be creative with our limited resources. I wanted my mother to teach me things and to spend time with me. Of course, I had grandma; but she was all of our grandmother. When my mother did visit us, I remember sharing her time, fighting with my sister for her attention, and detesting the moment she would leave us. I had an intense love for her, even if our relationship was built on sporadic visits.

In that three-story row home on Newkirk Street, my childhood was built on disconnectedness, disillusionment, and disappointment. I felt no connection to my mother and father.

I felt only an intense desire for a better relationship. I wanted to be held and spoiled and disciplined. I wanted to wake up to my mother's love. I wanted my father to visit me often. I wanted to tell him stories about school and about my friends and about the things that I was learning. I wanted to share my stories with my mother and father. I felt disappointment that my mother and father were out living their lives, while I was left to share those stories with my grandmother and aunt.

It wasn't until I learned to read and write that I stopped feeling like a mistake. My words and thoughts becomes a mirror of the experiences I had lived. Composition notebooks are more than journals, they are my amusement, my emotional release, and in many ways my best friend. If my words are a reflection of my generation, my words will tell a story of sadness, shame, and perseverance. My words will tell a story of struggle and progress. Writing has opened up my world. It has helped me understand myself and make sense of the complexities that exist in my world. It reassures me that I have purpose. Writing makes me feel important. My stories will be a mirror of the era in which I live.

◆ ◆ ◆ ◆ ◆

EIGHT
LOVE ON NEWKIRK STREET

Get your dirty behind back to Newkirk Street
And I better not catch you off that block
That block that street where all the fiends meet
Broken glass crack valves litter the concrete

I bet your momma get a welfare check
In her section eight home kids hanging from her neck
Isn't it five of yall, right?
You probably had to fight?
For a spot to lay your head
You probably share a bed?

Get your dirty behind back to Newkirk Street
And I better not catch you off that block

That block that street where all the fiends meet

Broken glass crack valves litter the concrete

People all up in your business

Abandoned homes and treeless

Most of yall probably fatherless

And your mother probably jobless,

Drugged up, depressed and hopeless

I heard Newkirk Street is loveless.

Get your dirty behind back to Newkirk Street

And I better not catch you off that block

That block that street where all the fiends meet

Broken glass crack valves litter the concrete

They say she stole her house

Her boyfriend molested her kids and she still stayed with him

Why in the God's name did she stay with him

She ain't pay her electricity bill

He ain't pay his water

She ain't pay her gas bill

Get your dirty behind back to Newkirk Street

And I better not catch you off that block

That block that street where all the fiends meet
Broken glass crack valves litter the concrete

Surrounded by nothing but sin
all roads leading to the pen
Or a dead-end, cause y'all hopeless
On a block that is Godless
I heard Newkirk Street was loveless.

◆ ◆ ◆ ◆ ◆

NINE
SUSPENDED

Today I am suspended from school. Mrs. Lewis caught me horse-playing in the hallway. Ironically, this time I wasn't even doing much. I've developed a reputation of having a hot temper with the tendency to end disputes violently.

One time, I punched an older student in the face because he called my sister a "bitch." His name was Kevin. Kevin was in my sister Sydney's class. She must have made Kevin upset or perhaps he was teasing her for no reason at all. I didn't even wait to learn the details.

When school let out, I saw my sister Sydney crying and upset. Then a few feet away there was Kevin. She complained saying he was roasting her and calling her names.

"What did he call you?" I asked.

"He called me a bitch."

"He must want an ass whooping," I said.

"There he go right there," Sydney said pointing at Kevin.

Kevin grinned as if he didn't care about Sydney's feelings. In our neighborhood, calling a female the "B" word was unacceptable. In fact, this word meant trouble. As Sydney's brother, it was my duty to protect her. Even if the other person was older and bigger, I had to defend my sister's honor.

As soon as we cleared school grounds, I dropped my backpack and stepped right to Kevin's face.

"What did you say to my sister?"

"Lil' boy, if you don't back up out of my face."

"What are you going to do?" I asked as we stood face to face.

Kevin dropped his backpack, which to me indicated he was ready to fight. Ding, ding, ding! I punched Kevin right in the face. Immediately a crowd formed around us. He punched me. Despite his age and size advantage, I had the upper hand. I was stronger and more experienced at fighting. I had been wrestling and fighting my whole life. Although we were exchanging blows, Kevin attempted to grab me, but I pushed him down to the ground.

A few guys rushed in to break up the fight. My sister Sydney pulled my arm and yelled at me to stop. I listened because she's the older sibling and because she never asked for me to protect her. We never got caught for that fight. And I'm proud to say Sydney never had a problem with Kevin again.

Fortunately for me, this time I was only caught horse playing. I'm grateful too because tussling bouts could easily escalate to fights.

While chess proved to be meaningful, I decided early that it is not for me. Scooter on the other hand, he excels at chess. Me on the other hand, I am not competitive or patient enough to sit through the long games. I like Mr. El and I appreciate Mrs. Lewis, but I can't resist the urge to act out.

Thankfully, this is only a one-day suspension. Tomorrow I may return to school without a parent. I'm glad because grandma has said she's had enough of me causing trouble at school. Even though I'm a smart student, I was never the best behaved in class. I am guilty of mimicking teachers, trying to hit classmates with pencils, and walking out of the class. I think my misbehavior now has much more to do with me finally making friends. Being in seventh grade is all about making friends and fitting in.

I'm grateful to get through the anger I had for so many years. When I was young, I showed my anger at home and on the playground. I would fight my sisters and cousin. I would confront the neighborhood boys for no reason. I even stabbed a classmate in the eye with a pencil. So much anger and rage because I felt ashamed.

I was angry because I couldn't cope with the absence of my parents. I was angry because I had no comfort and I had to share my space. I didn't even feel comfortable talking about my feelings with people. To me, no one understands me. The only privacy I have is writing. And since I still have this anger inside, it is important that I write.

A few years ago when I was in the fifth grade, one counselor suggested I start writing my thoughts. Her thinking was that it may help me feel better inside and it is a more healthy way to get my anger out. Ever since then, I've been writing.

◆ ◆ ◆ ◆ ◆

TEN

LOVE IS A LESSON

I decided to apply to one of the writing contest Ms. Sample gave me. The Scholastic Art and Writing Awards was my first choice because it has an impressive legacy dating back to 1923, not to mention a noteworthy roster of past winners, among them included Andy Warhol, Sylvia Plath, and Truman Capote.

I also want to participate in the contest to challenge my writing skills, but more importantly I wanted to impress Ms. Sample. I wanted her to know that I took her suggestion seriously. Moreover, the writing contest is an important opportunity for me to be recognized for my creativity.

I also would like for my work to be published. It would make my family and my teachers proud to see me participate in something positive, instead of always being disciplined for misbehavior and for fighting.

All I think about is love and I only write about love. I write about the love that is present, the love that is unaccounted for and the love that is found. I guess I feel that way because for a long time I felt I lacked love. I was taught not to be weak. And I was teased when I cried.

"Zion, stop that whining boy." I recall my grandma saying.

For as long as I remember, I was angry and confused. I felt I was the product of a misshapen miserable mother and a frightenedly fickle father. My grandma raised me because my mother and my father abandoned me. They left me in the care of my grandma. And for most of my childhood, I sought to understand why. It was difficult for me to understand how two adults could leave their child behind. I didn't understand.

But now that I'm thirteen, I completely understand why. I've been through enough to know right and know wrong. I've participated in enough programs to recognize what's best for me. I've read enough in school to recognize the themes and patterns of my own life.

When my counselor suggested I write about whatever I felt instead of taking out my frustrations on people, I began keeping my thoughts and experiences in marble composition books. I keep them stashed away in a Nike box under my bed.

These composition books are guardians of my thoughts and experiences. My writings have a lot to say about the power of love and the power of the written word. The written word has immense power. We activate that power when we listen to our hearts and permit our ideas, feelings, and experiences to manifest onto the page. Because I do not trust the people in my life, I must write in these books.

I am on a journey to discover the love in all situations and circumstances, whether pleasant or painful. When I encounter love it is important to analyze, synthesize, categorize, and otherwise process or make sense of love.

I laugh out loud when I think about how much time I spend writing in these books. I hope no one finds them. And if someone reads them, I hope it is only with my permission.

And I dare someone to call these journals "diaries." When I think about the word "diary," I imagine a twelve-year-old girl writing about how angry her day was or complaining about her friends or the unrequited love of a boy.

I tend to think that I am much smarter than that. My teachers would say that I do not pay attention in class, but the truth is I am a wanderer. I am always thinking about my thinking. And I am always analyzing my surroundings.

When I write I commit myself to open up emotionally, intellectually, and spiritually. I try to carry a composition book with me at all times. If I cannot get to a book, I write on whatever I can get my hands on.

Some of my writings found life on the back of receipts. Some of my writings I begin on Sticky Notes. Some of my writings are poems or love notes to my first crush Ashley. And some of my writings came about in a dream and actualized from my fantasy state. Certainly, I dream often. I try to remember my dreams so that when I regain consciousness I can attempt to dissect every image, thought, and feeling experienced in my dreams. And when I write, I carefully recognize and celebrate the love in all of my experiences. I like to write essays, stories and even poems, because often times, love is best expressed in the spontaneity of a poem.

Through writing about our experiences, we become equally human and equally vulnerable. My life is not rosy and I write to understand and hopefully overcome obstacles.

So I share my experiences with my journals. I address my childhood and my relationship with my family and my friends. Through writing I am learning to love myself, even if my parents didn't show me love. Writing helps me express my frustrations, because for a long time I was angry. I did not know how to control or channel those feelings, yet writing has taught me to acquire power and meaning in my life.

♦ ♦ ♦ ♦ ♦

ELEVEN
ABANDONED

Now that I've told the stories of my home and my name, it is time for me to share the story of how my mother and father abandoned me. I always lived with grandma. I can't remember ever living with my mother or my father.

Looking back, I have no recollection of my mother having a home for me to go to. She always lived with male friends or with relatives. My mother struggles with drug addiction. I guess matters got so bad that she became unfit to raise us. I guess it was her criminal history or the fact that she didn't have steady employment. I don't even know what my mother is good at.

When it comes to my father, I don't have many memories of him. And like most young boys, I always wanted to spend time with my father. When I was very young I remember longing for a relationship. I always wanted to get to know him as a person and to share stories with my father.

I remember I was doing exceptionally well in school. I was maybe in the fourth or fifth grade. I wanted my father to know that he had a good son. I wanted him to know that I was smart and I was a good writer. I wanted to make him proud. So I decided to ask my family what they knew about him.

I didn't know much about my father. I only knew that I didn't share the same father as my four older siblings. When my four siblings would leave out to spend time with their father, I would stay home with my grandma. She was intentional about making me feel valued during these times. She would take me to the barbershop or I would join her on errands. I knew I was loved, but I wanted to be loved by my father.

I remember my father visiting us when I was younger, but I never understood why I had a different father. I don't think the adults in my family considered it important. No one sat me down and explained to me, "Zion, you have a different father than your big brother and sisters." And no one sat me down to say, "Zion, let me tell you the story of your mother and father." I met my father maybe two or three times when I was much younger but now that I'm older I expect to know the truth.

One day, I decided to ask my mother the story of my father. My mother told me the truth about my father. My mother had been with my siblings' father for most of her young adult life. In fact, she says that she was in love with their father. She met my father during one of their breakups and became pregnant with me. According to her, she was never serious about my father. Her hopes were that he would make an effort to be a part of my life, despite his feelings or opinions for my mother.

He decided not to participate in my life. My mother was no better because she put drugs before her responsibilities.

◆ ◆ ◆ ◆ ◆

To Love, from Zion

TWELVE

DREAMS UNFULFILLED

Nightmares have a funny way of taking over my dreams. I had a good day yesterday. And when I have good days I tend to have good dreams. But for some strange reason I found myself trapped in a cycle of nightmares. In the first dream, I imagined grandma dying. Of course, I was heart-broken and confused. I cried in my dream. It was one of the rare occasions when our family was together. But it was only a bad dream. I turned over as if I was changing the channel of my mind.

In the second nightmare, a violent gang was chasing me through the neighborhood. They were randomly attacking innocent people. I witnessed them brutally attack a woman. I couldn't help her because they were too many and I was alone. All I had was my speed. I ran as fast as I could go and as far as I could see. I ran myself to consciousness and woke up panting, gasping for air. I was out of breath.

When I woke up, I couldn't go back to sleep. I got a drink of water. I went to check on grandma. I stuck my head in her room. Grandma was still awake.

"Zion, that's you?" She asked.

"Yes ma'am," I replied.

"Go back to bed," she commanded.

I did as instructed. When I returned to my room, I had to force myself to sleep. I start by counting. And then I try to imagine good thoughts: the more pleasant the better. So tonight, I'm going to dream about my mother.

Right now, all I can think about is my mother. Despite her abandonment, I love my mom no matter what she does, no matter what happens. I call it my momma's love. That night I dreamt of my mother and when I woke up, I decided to write. Writing seems to be the best way for me to communicate my feelings in my mother's absence. Since she's not physically here with me daily, I find myself writing about the relationship I wish we had.

Whenever I look at mother, I smile because I know she loves me. Despite the circumstances of her absences, I know at night she prays to God and ask that he take care of me. I know that she's proud of what she's produced. I know when she cries her tears are of joy, love, and pride. I love my mother, I got my momma's love.

The other day, my Social Studies teacher, Mrs. Donovan-Snavely, asked me, "How'd you become such a polite young man?" I told her mommy taught me. She taught me to open doors for women, walk on the outer path of the street, and to never say "hate." "Hate" is not a good word. My teacher smiled because she knows I love my momma, I got my momma's love.

I got my momma's love in the morning when I wake to pray to the Lord. I got my momma's love when I'm in trouble; she gives me strength to go on. I got my momma's love; she keeps my back up straight. I got my momma's love at night when I pray to God, asking that He always watch over her and protect her from harm. I love my momma. I got my momma's love.

My momma keeps me whole. She keeps me just right. I can see her in me when I look in the mirror at night. Despite her neglect, I can never be mad at her. Let me repeat that point, despite her neglect, I can never be mad at her. I owe her everything no matter what she does. Because when I am mad, she makes me happy. And when I am down, she brings me up again. Momma is here with me even when she is not. I love mommy; I got my momma's love.

When I was young I would cry for mommy. I would wish she were there for me, so she could hold me. No one could hold me like mommy holds me. And when my momma held me, it felt so warm. I had peace in my momma's arms. Grandma and Aunt Helena would tell me, "She'll be right back." I'd cry because I felt incomplete and I wanted mommy near.

Grandma would love me and hold me in her arms, tell me "it's going to be fine." And kiss me on the head.

Aunt Helena would give me something good to eat and the nutrients I needed to grow strong. And still there was no one who could hold me the way my momma holds me. Because mommy gives me peace and mommy keeps me warm. I love mommy, I got my momma's love.

You see it is hard to remember because I was just a little boy. I can tell you a few of the things mommy and I would do together. Mommy and I would sing songs. She had the ability to change her voice producing the cutest sounds. Mommy would test my knowledge of reading and arithmetic. So I made sure I learned something new every time she was around.

Anxious to make her proud, I would shout, "guess what I know?" And she always smiled. I love mommy, I got my momma's love.

These dreams conjure up the most rare and intimate memories I have of my parents. I remember one time we rode the 15-trolley to my father's house. It was always fun to ride the bus, especially with momma. We could ride forever. The trolley would bump and our butts would jump from our seats. And when we got there my dad would have that real deep voice and he never said much. He'd only ask my momma questions and I would stand there holding momma's hand. He was the unknown to me. Yet despite the distance, I loved my father. I wanted him to know me. And likewise I wanted to know him. I wanted him to take me to school.

I wanted him to pick me up and throw me up into the air. But that was never happening. He took me to the Green Garden Chinese Store to get some food. We had shrimp fried rice and chicken with broccoli. We at in the living room. I sat on the floor in front of the coffee table while we watched tv. He barely said a word.

One Saturday, my mother came over to see me. I can remember her running in our house to tell my grandma she was taking me to see Sam. Momma then put a coat over me, picked me up and ran outside. There on 29th and Girard Avenue we'd meet my father for only a brief second. He would give momma some money and put some more in my hand. Then we'd watch Sam get right back on the 15-trolley and I wouldn't see him for another couple of months.

Mommy wasn't always there, but I know she wanted to be there. I knew she tried. She always told me good things. I never knew why she didn't live with us. I never knew why I didn't see her all of the time. All I know is that I needed her close to me. Every time she was there for me I cherished every moment. Now I know the reasons.

And I want mommy to be right. I want my sisters and my brother to be able to hold each other with mommy in the middle. I want us to have a family picture. I want mommy to be able to cook a good meal for all of us to eat. I want mommy to treat us all like we were still her little babies. I want her to have a house where I can come home to. I want her to see how much I lover her. I want her to see all the love I have for our family. I want her to make us strong. I want her to see that momma's love inside of me.

◆ ◆ ◆ ◆ ◆

THIRTEEN
LEARNED LESSONS

On any given weekend, you can find me at home with my siblings. I have three older sisters and one older brother. I am the youngest of five. We grew up close and we shared everything. We shared a room, each other clothes, and even our beds. For most of our lives we slept two to a bed. We attended the same schools. We had the same teachers. We participated in the same groups and clubs.

We thought alike. At times, we finished one another thoughts. We went to school together, went to church together, we sang together, and we studied together. We auditioned together for school plays and for choir roles. And consequently competition was a part of our lives. Our togetherness strengthened us in so many ways. Grandma exposed us to many opportunities in our childhood.

Often when our mother would visit we would do our best to win over her attention. We equally love our mother, but show her love differently. In the same ways that we were the same, we were also different. My sisters America and India were mouthy and talkative. Sydney was sneaky and sensitive. My brother Zaire and I were both quick witted and sarcastic. We used our words like weapons. We fought often. We argued constantly. We did everything together. We watched television together. We played games together. We acted out together. We were spectators. We absorbed the world in its entirety as one.

We learned lessons together and from the mistakes of one another. My older siblings learned the hardest lessons. Unexpected pregnancies, middle school and high school dropouts, and drug dealing were all lessons I didn't have to learn because my siblings had already taught me how not to be. Seeing their experiences and their struggles motivated me to do things differently.

◆ ◆ ◆ ◆ ◆

FOURTEEN
FOR ZAIRE

My brother and I don't have the best relationship. We get along well with one another. But in my heart, I wish we were closer. Nevertheless, I am grateful. So for the writing competition, I decided to submit a poem dedicated to my brother Zaire.

I was excited to share my poem with the world. When I got to school, instead of going directly to homeroom, I went to Ms. Sample's class to share my poem.

"Ms. Sample, check out my poem," I said. "I wrote it for the Scholastic writing competition."

"That's great Zion," Ms. Sample said. "Let me take a look at it." I handed her the poem from the same folder she had given me. Her eyes widened as they moved across and down the page.

"Zion, stand over here." Ms. Sample pointed to the front of the classroom. I stood where she told me.

"Recite the poem aloud," Ms. Sample said. "The spoken word brings the poem to life. I would love to hear it from your voice." She handed the poem back to me.

Now that I've grown, I can better see.
How good you've been to me.
I'm blessed to have what some others do not have
An angel to guide me along the way.
Eyes when I cannot see,
Ears when I cannot hear
Legs when I cannot walk, and a
Voice when I cannot speak
An angel to insure me when I'm feeling ill

I know I can rely on you.
Though I may not call all of the time
or write when I'm away
I am always thinking of you everyday.
Remembering the past which we will always share.

I remember when it was your thirteenth birthday
And your godmother gave you one hundred dollars.
You took me with you downtown.
We went to The Gallery and you bought me two action
figures, Cable and Wolverine from the X-Men
It was a day that I'd always remember.
Then we went to the food court and had pizza.
I don't remember all of the details but I do remember that I
was happy.
There are the little things in life that we never forget.

I'm proud of you no matter what.
Hold on to your faith and God will take care of you.
I'll always love you.
You are my big brother my only brother a true blessing from God.

You are my strength, my eyes, my ears, my voice,
my legs when I cannot walk.
I am a reflection of you.
So whatever I've become you've also become.

Instead of clapping, Ms. Sample simply smiled and snapped her fingers three times. She reached her hand out for the poem.

"So you like it," I asked.

"Oh of course, Zion," she said. "I think it was a great idea to write a poem for your brother. By doing so, you've given it purpose far greater than just the writing competition. This is something you can share with your family, even if you do not win." Ms. Sample made a great point. I appreciated her guidance.

"What motivates you to write, Zion?" Ms. Sample asked.

"Well," I thought about the question. "School of course. I have to write in school."

"And what else?" she asked. Ms. Sample studied me with her eyes. I understood her questions, but I guess the only other person that showed interest in my writing was grandma. I didn't want to tell her that I write because sometimes I feel no one wants to listen. I didn't want to tell her that I write to cope with the fact that my mother isn't around.

"I just enjoy writing," I said.

Ms. Sample held up the submission form. "I'm going to fill this out for you and submit your poem to the competition. All forms of literacy is important in my opinion: reading and writing. Try to remember what motivates you to write. And whenever you feel comfortable, I would love to hear about it."

◆ ◆ ◆ ◆ ◆

FIFTEEN

MAGICAL BLACK BOOK

That evening, I gave Ms. Sample's words much thought. It made more sense to me when grandma walked through the door from her Bible study class. It clicked. Grandma is the reason I love to write.

I remember people's reactions from reading that black book with gold pages in church. I remember how they would recite the words and lines in unison. And I remember how they would respond with "Mmms," "Amens," and "Hallelujahs." My grandmother would take my brother, sisters and I to church with her every Friday and Sunday.

From as far back as I remember I recall being somewhat involved with my grandmother's church. I say her church because I really didn't have much choice. She obviously wanted us to know her God. I was the youngest of five. My older siblings would hold their Bibles during scripture readings and I would mimic them. When the older women would catch the Holy Spirit I watched with awe and was always curious about how God actually chose them to bless their legs and feet and cause them to shout. Grandma could have left us five at home with my Aunt Helena. Yet I am glad she woke up early dressed us and took us to church with her because she exposed me to my first understandings of literacy.

Literacy for me was the connection and relationship the people in that church felt with their Bibles. They ingested and consumed those words. My grandmother would put on her glasses and recite the words jubilantly and I saw a total difference from the stern and strict woman I knew at home. She was only five foot two, but I believe she is the strongest person in the world. And if she loved that book so should her little grandson.

I was a little boy that loved to sing. The church introduced me to some of my first songs. After the people read from the black book, they would pick up the red book. I knew then that it was time to sing. "This is the day, this is the day that the lord has made, that the lord has made. Let us rejoice and be glad in it." Oh I loved that song. My grandmother kept me by her side. I would clap my hands and tap my feet emulating her movements and expressions. I would later come to learn that the red book was the church's Hymnal.

My grandmother's religion and spiritual expression inspired me to become more literate so I could better understand the mysticism I observed on Sundays. She was everything to me. She raised me as a baby when my mother wasn't there. She provided my siblings and me with all of the things we needed. But she was tough and she would beat us when we broke a rule or got into fights. Yet during her spiritual moments or while she was in church she would affectionately express her love for us. Sometimes she would convey this by softly patting my head and smiling or with candy from a sandwich bag in her purse. On Sundays, grandma would occasionally make breakfast, which made us all immensely excited. And as a young boy, I knew that those books had a great deal of influence on her.

I knew then that these two books held great and mysterious power. I wanted to know that power like my grandma knew it. And when I was old enough, grandma began taking me to bible study. It would just be one of my sisters and me, my other siblings too proud or too full of themselves to be dragged to church with grandma. But I loved hearing the stories from that black book. I loved the songs from the red hymnal. I loved seeing how people connected with those books. Most of all I loved experiencing those magical moments with my grandmother.

◆ ◆ ◆ ◆ ◆

SIXTEEN
THREE DAYS TO SEE

I gradually realized that I should share my writing with others and that I shouldn't be ashamed. The more I reflect on all of my experiences the more appreciative I become. For example, today Ms. Sample is teaching a lesson on Helen Keller. The essay is called "Three Days to See." As Ms. Sample prepared us for the reading selection, I took a glance at the assignment. The hook to Ms. Sample's lesson was "how would you live each day if you were to die tomorrow." As soon as I read those words, a plethora of thoughts raced through my mind.

I said to Scooter, "it reminds me of twenty-four hours to live, right."

"Oh my goodness, it does," Scooter agreed.

"All right!" Ms. Sample snapped at me. "Go ahead Zion, you read." Then she held up the assignment. What I liked most about this class is that Ms. Sample did not show favoritism. A class disruption was a class disruption.

Ashley grinned at me. The entire class paused awaiting Ms. Sample's next instructions. I wasn't sure if I should begin reading or if she simply wanted me to stop talking while she instructed. So I read.

"Helen Keller was an American author, political activist, and lecturer," I read. Since learning to read, I was taught to read with enthusiasm. Sometimes I would even adjust my voice to the tone of the writing. "Keller was born with the ability to see and hear, but at 19 months old she contracted an illness which left her deaf and blind. The story of how Keller's teacher, Anne Sullivan, taught her sign language and helped her communicate has become widely known through the play and film *The Miracle Worker*. The following excerpt comes from Keller's autobiography." Ms. Sample told me to pause. Then she handed Scooter a stack of papers.

"Pass these out please," she instructed. "You may continue to read Zion." I continued to read while Scooter passed out the discussion questions.

Ms. Sample asked me to pause again. She said, "as you read, take notes on how Helen Keller describes her learning process and pay attention to how she values each day." We continued reading independently until Ms. Sample instructed us to start answering the text-dependent questions. She allowed us to work collaboratively in answering the questions until the bell rang.

The irony and timing of this lesson is so profound because my friends and I can't stop listening to a rap song named "24 Hours to Live," by Mase featuring The Lox and Black Rob. In fact, Jamaal and I repeatedly blast Mase's *Harlem World* album. And Scooter and I have memorized all of the verses and lines of the song. We often go back and forth between our favorite verses. Despite its gritty and grimy lyrics and the fact that the song was about death, we liked hardcore rap music. The more violent the better.

The overall message of the song is what would you do with your last day on earth. Ms. Sample assigned us homework and an essay assignment due next week. For homework we are to make a list of some of the things we take for granted, and answer the discussion questions about Helen Keller's essay. The essay assignment is to write about how would you live each day if you were to die tomorrow.

Before the bell rang, Ms. Sample asked me to stay for a minute. As the class dismissed, Ms. Sample handed me a large white envelope.

"Congratulations Zion," she said. "Your poem was selected for the Philadelphia Writing Project Scholastic Art and Writing Awards. You received honorable mention and this certificate."

I opened the envelope and read.

Congratulations Zion Major! Your poem For Zaire has been chosen as Honorable Mention for this year's Philadelphia Writing Project Scholastic Art and Writing Awards. You are a writer. We believe your words are powerful and would love to share them with the world. Your submission will be published in our winner's journal coming this summer.

I was excited but grateful that Ms. Sample kept my success a secret. I would not have been proud if she announced it to the entire class. "Thank you," I said.

I raced home to tell grandma. But she wasn't home yet. Instead, my Aunt Helena was doing someone's hair. I didn't mention it. In fact, I just said "hello" to everyone and sat on the living room floor and began my homework assignment.

◆ ◆ ◆ ◆ ◆

SEVENTEEN

SPONGE ON THE LIVING ROOM FLOOR

While growing up, I was exposed to that kind of talk that goes on among women. It was my grandma, my Aunt Helena, my sisters America, India, and Sydney. We were always in the house together. My older brother would run the streets. He could hang out with friends, play basketball at the recreation center, or stand on the corners with the older neighborhood boys.

My aunt made a living braiding and styling women's hair. In our living room, she would position her clients comfortably in front of the television. It was the only television we could use in the house.

On most days she would have women waiting to be served since she was very efficient with her small but quick fingers. Each and every customer would sit for an hour to sometimes four hours telling stories, debating, and reliving moments in their lives. As the youngest and in need of the most supervision, I would sit right in the living room absorbing it all.

I heard their stories about work, drama, fashion, other women, men, religion, politics, entertainment and probably most of all gossip. I would sit there watching the only television available to me, since I couldn't watch TV in my grandma's room unless she was home–or be subjected to watch her Soap Operas, which she affectionately called "the stories."

Aunt Helena would work as expeditiously as possible all the while entertaining her clients with television, snacks, and Newport cigarettes. She would occasionally pause to take a five-minute Newport break, smoke her cigarette, tend to her children, and take a sip of Sunkist, her favorite drink. I would sit silently facing the television pretending to be invisible. Most of the time I felt that way. I was always greeted by her clients but only really engaged when I was asked to run an errand or go to the store.

The women always loved me though; they thought I was respectful and well mannered. As they sat and talked about everything under the sun, I would absorb everything under the sun, particularly their stories.

The television told fantastical stories and projected lifestyles I knew were out of my grasp. But the stories I heard daily by these women were real. Whether consciously or subconsciously, I admire Aunt Helena for exposing me to such stories. Nevertheless, I had little choice or control and perhaps that accounts for me pretending to blend in with the furniture. I quietly sat.

I am Aunt Helena's youngest nephew, but after me came her children London, Lydia, Lateefah, Mashaad, and Messiah. And since she was like a second mother to me, her children were my younger siblings. The closest in age with me was her first child, London. We are only four months apart. London's father was extremely involved in his life, unlike my father.

I spent more time with my Aunt Helena than I spent with my own mother and father. Grandma was my legal guardian, but she worked hard to make sure we had everything we needed. When grandma was at work, at church, or handling a house-full of responsibilities I was left in the care of Aunt Helena. Despite her fussing, nagging, and complaining about the world, I value the stories and the lessons learned while I sat on the living room floor.

◆ ◆ ◆ ◆ ◆

To Love, from Zion

EIGHTEEN
MOTHER MONSTER

The lessons continued on the neighborhood streets. The most common denominator in our hood is single mothers. Almost all of my friends live with just their mothers. No fathers, just an occasional boyfriend or quasi-stepdad. When I think of my two friends Jamaal and Sam, the reality is we teach one another about the world. We learn from one another what it means to be a man, what it means to be a friend, and what it means to be a brother. "What's up, bro?" I always greeted my friends with bro.

"What's up?" Jamaal said.

"How long y'all been out here." I asked.

"Maybe like twenty minutes," Sam said.

"Cool."

Today, like most days, Jamaal, Sam, and I are just sitting on the corner steps. We watch the neighborhood and the people coming and going. People rushing to catch the bus to work. Children collecting coins for chips and candy. Single mothers yelling at their children to go outside and play. I love the city because there's so much to learn and to see. We watch Bo, the neighborhood car washer. As he washes car after car, we observe how efficiently he works. Although Bo is in his late thirties and still lives with his mother, we young bucks still show him respect. We never talked about Bo's work ethic. We simply watched him work.

"What's going on out here on these streets?" Sam would ask.

"What you mean?" I said.

"Who gave these young girls permission to get pregnant?" Sam asked jokingly.

"I know man," Jamaal added. "It's like every eighth grade girl is competing on who can get pregnant first."

"It's like a competition," I added. "Even my sister is pregnant. All of these young girls out here pregnant."

"It's like children having children," Jamaal said. We talk about issues. We talked about what we see. All throughout our neighborhood there were young mothers.

We recognized the pattern of poverty in the neighborhood. When one generation fails they conspire to ruin their own children. They teach their children to be lazy, unmotivated, and dependent. It hurts to see these young women. I call them mother monsters. So I decided to write a poem.

Mother monster teach me your way
Show me how to devour what I see
Consume and waste.
Mother monster allow the world to use me as it pleases
Share me with the world, while you have your way
Mother monster be my monster mother
Create a monstrous self-reflecting image in your likeness
Monstrous mother let me shake my booty, roll my eyes
Speak ill and be as monstrous as I want to be
Never talk with me, play with me
Just let the world use me like a sponge
Soaking in your filthy ways
Mother monster make me like you
A manifestation of your monstrous ways

There are many ways to raise a monster. Bad parents have been successful at raising monsters. I am not sure if these women even understand. Their actions are unjust and irreversible. We continued people watching and shooting the breeze. We stayed out until the street lights came on.

Later that evening, I decide to share with grandma my poems, but particularly my accomplishment. I showed grandma the envelope Ms. Sample gave me.

"What an achievement, Zion!" grandma said.

"Thank you," I said. I held my composition notebook in my hand. I had so much more to share. Grandma could tell.

"I don't have money or great things to give you, but what I can give to you is knowledge and the truth," grandma said. "You got sense boy, so you better use it."

And let's be clear your mother is not a monster.

She's just done a monstrous thing by putting drugs before her children. Neglect is a monstrous thing.

"Yes, I understand ma'am," I said. "But it hurts because I want her love."

I didn't expect the conversation to go in this direction. But it was clear, my writing choices gave us much to reflect on. Grandma had a lot on her heart. She had to share with me how she felt.

"We all want love Zion," she continued. "And I'm doing my best to provide love to you, your brother, and your sisters. But it's not easy because I thought I was done raising kids." I understood grandma's perspective. This conversation was long overdue. I knew grandma was proud of my accomplishment. And I know she wants to see me continue to do better.

"I don't want you getting into trouble in school," she added. "It's good to see you doing positive things. You have to follow your own path. You have to tell your own story."

◆ ◆ ◆ ◆ ◆

To Love, from Zion

NINETEEN

ANXIETY

Definitely today was not my usual Thursday. To begin the day I woke up at about 7 AM to finish writing my test review. Being a natural procrastinator, I lost track of time and I was almost late to school.

Ms. Sample was calling to remind me to be on time. Today's exam would determine which high school I'm eligible to go to. The higher my scores the better my chances of getting into George Washington Carver High School. Grandma had noticed my diligence and had been praying for me.

When I got to school, I saw Scooter who had appeared to be confident about this upcoming exam. "What's up Scooter?" I asked.

Scooter just nodded and got up. Then he paced the floor looking inside our homeroom. "Man I'm just ready to get this test over with!" He exclaimed finally.

We shared the same anxiety. I just chuckled and replied. "Bro, you and me both." As we waited, I peeked my head inside the room where students were finishing their exams from the previous class.

Standardized test causes me so much anxiety. Teachers had been drilling us with strategies and reading material but I didn't follow along with the class.

I started to study the day before the exam. Yet I'll admit I'm feeling extremely anxious to get this started. The only trouble I had was on one of the reading passages. It was an extremely dull article about pesticides. I didn't answer all of the questions.

I also forgot to use the bathroom before the test so within forty minutes my legs were shaking in an attempt to hold my pee. I had to go bad and I knew I wouldn't be allowed to use the bathroom during the exam. I know I passed and I left the room in confidence.

It is weird how I could be so filled with anxiety and then come out of the test feeling confident. It is a war in my mind. I am not a very good test taker. In fact, I hate tests. I love writing and I want to become a writer one day. I just hate that school is so much about test. It's all that seems to matter any more.

I am even more excited that things can go back to normal again. The school year is ending soon. And I'm grateful for free-time, basketball, and hanging out.

◆ ◆ ◆ ◆ ◆

To Love, from Zion

TWENTY
THE REINSTATEMENT
HEARING

Middle school is proving to be a challenge for me. I am always angry. I keep getting into fights and I am being very disrespectful to my teachers. At seventh grade, I've probably been suspended at least six times, not to mention the pink slips.

And now I'm suspended again for fighting another boy. I had a very short temper. One thing I do not tolerate is other boys talking about my mother. This particular boy had the misfortune of learning the hard way. He not only called me dirty, but he also called my mother a "crack-head." In a fit of rage, I punched the boy right in the face. When he swung back at me, I proceeded to pound on his face and body with both fists.

Fights had the power to incite a crowd. And this incident certainly got the attention of all of my schoolmates, the noontime aids, and school officials. I was taken to the assistant principal's office and suspended.

"Zion, I am tired of seeing you in my office," Mrs. Lewis said. Mrs. Lewis was one of three assistant principals at Vaux Middle School. She had many conversations with me throughout the year regarding my misbehavior. Some of those conversations took place during student teacher conferences. Mrs. Lewis had had enough.

She called my grandmother at work. I could not hear her responses, but I knew how this conversation would go once I saw her at home later that day. After Mrs. Lewis got off of the phone, called for a school police officer on her walkie-talkie. While we waited for the school police officer, Mrs. Lewis took the opportunity to express her frustrations with me.

She stared at me for about fifteen seconds and analyzed me. She finally broke her silence. "Zion, what's going on?" she asked.

Not knowing what to actually say or even how to describe some of my problems, I decided not to say anything at all.

"Nothing," I replied.

"Well, there has to be something wrong with you. You keep getting into trouble and this is your sixth time getting suspended," she said.

I simply shrugged my shoulders. "I don't know," I said.

"Well, you're smart and capable of much more," she said. "I'm going to send you home today. Here are your suspension papers. I already notified your grandmother that you have a two-day suspension. In order to be reinstated, a parent or guardian must bring you back for a conference. Understand?" "Yes, Ma'am," I said.

The five-block walk home took all of fifteen minutes. The lonely saunter gave me an opportunity to reflect. My grandmother worried about my anger problems. She had witnessed enough failure in our family. Perhaps it was the fact that I was the youngest and the most reachable, but I knew this suspension would disappoint her, yet again.

When I got home, I went straight to my room to avoid having to face grandma when she finally arrived home. I tried to force myself to dream of a future where I didn't have to experience these lectures. I imagined myself being the good student I used to be. I dreamt about being in control of my emotions and not allowing others to get the best of me. I did not want to disappoint her or endure another lecture.

I finally fell asleep to fantasies of living in a big home with all of my family.

"Get up, boy!" shouted grandma. She shook my shoulder and I turned my head to face her. Grandma glared at me with a face full of fury. "I told you the last time you were suspended, that I wasn't coming back up to that school again."

Grandma could be very straightforward sometimes. This incident was no exception. However, I was really expecting a lecture and maybe even an opportunity to explain myself. My rest was only momentarily interrupted, because grandma really did not have much to say.

"Ask your mother if she can take you back up to the school," she added. I knew by her blatant disregard for the details of my most recent suspension that she was fed up. She did not ask me any questions. I could sense her frustration and disappointment. It pained me to know that I was causing grandma more stress and heartache. But I also knew that trying to apologize or explain what happened would not be effective. I had no real reason to be in this situation. Someone said something to me and I completely overreacted. There was no excuse as to why I put my hands on another individual. I was embarrassed and ashamed all over again.

On the day my mother was to reinstate me at school, I saw my grandmother off to work. She instructed me that my mother was to meet me at around 9am. We would have to walk to the school. I already understood this. I usually walked to school anyway. But I imagine she was telling me this for communication purposes. She wanted something to say before she left for work. Or perhaps she could sense my trepidation.

She kissed me on the forehead and said "see you later." I sat and waited patiently. The entire time trying to suppress the myriad of thoughts that danced through my mind. My absent mother was unpredictable and I did not know what to expect from today's reinstatement hearing.

I finally fell asleep to fantasies of living in a big home with all of my family. When suddenly the front door awakened me. It was my mother. She was wearing an oversized black dress. I sat up on the couch and massaged my resting eyes.

"Hey Boop," she said.

"Hi Mom," I replied.

As we walked to the school, I tried not to pay attention to the way my mother looked. But I could not put the way she smelled out of my mind. Her dress smelled of burnt oatmeal. It was black and oversized. I had a strong inclination that mother was high. And her appearance only added fuel to the fire. I was in this situation because a classmate teased me about my mother. The last thing I wanted was to be seen with her.

We walked to the school, signed into the front desk and were escorted to the assistant principal's office. I was embarrassed that my classmates would actually see my mother. I didn't want them to know that she was actually on drugs.

We waited in Mrs. Lewis's office to discuss my behavior and the circumstances for my suspension. When Mrs. Lewis actually arrived, she introduced herself to my mother. I did not lift my head. I was not proud and I was embarrassed. Mrs. Lewis could see my pain. She immediately began the conference. She read to my mother the write up and asked me if she got it right.

I nodded my head. She explained to my mother the consequence and asked my mother if she understood them. My mother said yes and she was told she could leave and that I would be reinstated immediately. Mrs. Lewis asked me to stay seated.

She directed my mother where to go while I waited patiently in the office. My mother left. Mrs. Lewis returned to her office. She sat down.

"Zion what's wrong with you," she asked.

My head sank deeper into my chest. I shrugged my shoulders.

"I can see that you're embarrassed," she said.

I started to cry. She reached for some Kleenex and handed them to me. I used the tissue to wipe my eyes and nose. I was overwhelmed. Mrs. Lewis could sense the energy in the room and perhaps that's why she kept the conference short. She pulled her chair closer to me.

"I know you love your mother," she said. "But you can't be angry about it either. You can't get into fights because people say things."

I nodded my head. And then she said the most profound thing that I have ever heard. "You can't want someone to do better or to change," she said. "You can't love them into changing. So you can love your mother all you want, but she has to want to change. So don't make it your responsibility."

Mrs. Lewis gave me much to reflect on. She knew I was upset about my relationship with my mother. We sat in the office and we talked about my mother. She helped me to realize that I should not make it my responsibility to change others. My mother has to be willing to change. We cannot make people do the things we want them to do, even if the thing we are asking of them is best for them.

◆ ◆ ◆ ◆ ◆

To Love, from Zion

TWENTY-ONE

POSSIBILITIES ARE LIMITLESS

Grandma does her best to motivate us all. She makes sure we are prepared for school and we have supplies. She makes sure we study and we behave in school.

Yet no matter how hard she works to motivate us, she still doesn't have what it takes to provide for us. Five growing teenagers require money, stability, and a college savings plan. Grandma and I have never talked about college. She understands that I want to go. And I understand that she wants the best for me. But it is clear that she doesn't understand what the best looks like for me.

Most parents expect their children to go to college. Savannah and Sam have never even had a conversation with me about school, let alone college. On the other hand, grandma has encouraged me to participate in chess and to write more. She wants me to go to Carver High School or to Girard Preparatory School. She says that these high schools will provide me with better opportunities than our neighborhood high school. I have the same goal and I don't want to be faced with the same challenges as my siblings or the neighborhood kids. Attending a better school would be the first practical step to preparing me for college.

We were told repeatedly by teachers and administrators to go to our school counselors when we needed help or advice. Now that the high school selection process was nearing, I gave much thought to the conversations grandma and I had and to my chances at being accepted into a good high school.

One day, I went into the counselor's office to talk with my assigned counselor, Mr. Pomerico. Mr. Pomerico was a white man in his mid thirties. He was well known at Vaux Middle School and well received by most of the students. We like him because he was laid back and seemed somewhat detached from his work responsibilities. I asked him if we could discuss the high school selection process.

"Sure Zion, have a seat," he said. And then he proceeded to get the latest booklet of high school listings and rankings. I sat down as instructed. His office was in disarray.

He put together many documents and placed the booklet with the documents in my hands.

Before I could say a word, Mr. Pomerico began talking. "Ben Franklin or William Penn High? Where do you see yourself?"

I frowned because I had not given neither Ben Franklin nor William Penn High a consideration. These were the two neighborhood schools my grandma warned me not to attend. I shook my head.

"Mr. Pomerico, I don't want to go to Ben Franklin or William Penn High," I said. "That's why I am here. I am here to discuss my chances at getting into Carver High School or into Girard Preparatory School."

Mr. Pomerico turned to his computer. Then he looked at me. "Zion, those schools accept the best. Have you seen their rankings. Those schools rank among the top in the city. Honestly with your test scores and your discipline record, you have no chance of getting into those schools. I think you should reconsider your options."

I was shocked and offended. I really wanted to jump from my seat and run out of his office. But I allowed him to finish. Being the stubborn person I am, I vowed not to confide in Mr. Pomerico anymore and I took my questions to our other counselor Mrs. McArthur.

Mrs. McArthur was a young black counselor. She graduated from Spelman College and had won the respect of students, teachers, and the administration. She was compassionate, energetic, and very attentive to her students' needs. She was not my assigned counselor but I felt confident she would work with me and assist me with my needs. She had a philosophy that all Vaux Middle School students were her students, even if they were not assigned to her.

I told Mrs. McArthur my intent on applying to Carver High School and to Girard Preparatory School. She smiled in agreement. Then I shared with her my experience with Mr. Pomerico. Mrs. McArthur had a different approach. Her philosophy was for me to set high goals and to do my best to work toward them. She encouraged me to apply to Carver High School and to Girard Preparatory School.

As a counselor, her expectations had a huge influence on what I expected of myself. Even if I wasn't the most qualified student and if I had discipline issues, it felt good to know that someone cares about me and my future. I did not dwell on Mr. Pomerico. It would be a waste of energy to focus on the negative. When people have faith in me and encourage me it makes feel like possibilities are limitless. It inspired me to write:

Possibilities are limitless
Put your mind's eye on the
sky, dive and watch
The entire world while
you're up high

Up so high, wish I could sky dive
On possibilities, are endless
if you dream big and hope for
something so more
But only if you work for

Possibilities are bountiful
plentiful, wonderful
So put your best two feet forward
Don't you dare be a slave to mediocrity
Don't you dare be a slave to complacency
Hope you grow don't you know
That you only evolve if you work hard

People like grandma, Mrs. McArthur, and Mrs. Lewis
helped me to envision my future at a time when the social
anxieties and opportunities of middle school loomed larger than
life.

◆ ◆ ◆ ◆ ◆

To Love, from Zion

TWENTY-TWO
BASKETBALL DREAMS

In our neighborhood, playing basketball was a right of passage. We played everyday. We played all day, until the lights came on. We played through the night in the Rec center's light.

We played until we were drenched in sweat. Then we'd walk home dehydrated allowing the cool wind to dry our sweat. All we did was talk and play basketball. You weren't considered cool unless you knew how to play basketball. My cousin London, and my two closest friends Jamaal and Sam were my basketball brothers. When we weren't talking and sitting on the stoop, we were playing basketball at the Athletic Recreation Center.

Everybody calls the Athletic Recreation Center, The Rec. It's at the corner of 26th and Masters Streets. The Rec is surrounded by the neighborhood elementary schools Kelly Elementary and Robert Morris Elementary and our middle school Robert Vaux Middle.

When it was just the three of us, we would play Twenty One, Rough House, Around the World, HORSE or PIG. These games were ideal because it was every man for himself, and no player has any teammates. Twenty-one was the simplest game, the winner being the first player to reach 21 points. Rough House was our favorite. This is another every man for himself game, the winner being the first person to score thirty-five points. Around the World was perfect for practicing your jump shot, because each player must make a series of shots arranged in and around the key. Then there was HORSE and PIG, which always became very competitive. The rules of the game are the first player chooses a spot on the court and takes a shot and if the shot is made, the next player must repeat the exact same shot. Jamaal always won. He was one of the best shooters in our neighborhood.

Jamaal was probably the best shooter on Newkirk Street. He had a weird shot, but it was textbook form. He knew that in order to perfect his jump shot, he had to follow through. Sam was the big man with the jump shot and crazy fade away. He could post you up and was great on collecting rebounds.

My cousin London had the most all-around skills. Whenever we were all together we made sure we played basketball as a team. We all expected to see London playing college basketball.

Games of one-on-one, two-on-two, and three-on-three, were always played half court. Four-on-four and five-on-five gave us a chance to play on the full court. We preferred playing full court because it made us feel like actual basketball players. We could fast break and correctly run plays that we had learned from watching the NBA and playing NBA 2K or NBA Live.

There was beauty and love in playing basketball with my boys. Not romantic love, but the brotherly love that comes when friends bond. We thought we were tough. We thought we had skills. We thought we had what it takes to be professionals. Essentially, we had basketball dreams.

◆ ◆ ◆ ◆ ◆

To Love, from Zion

TWENTY-THREE
SYDNEY'S NEGLECT

My sister Sydney caused our family much stress and heartache. Her being the youngest girl, my grandma devoted a great deal of time grooming her. She had been unsuccessful with my other sisters America and India. The two girls had accumulated many suspensions in school including fighting and using drugs. My grandma had had enough. She shipped my sisters north to a juvenile facility for troubled youth.

Despite recognizing the obvious signs that Sydney was headed in the same direction, my grandma refused to do the same with Sydney. All of Savannah's children had issues growing up, including myself. We were angry. We all acted out in school from time to time. And we all got into trouble in our neighborhood. Yet grandma continuously tried to keep us keep us whole. She was vigilant with Sydney and I because we are the youngest.

She would make us study at the dining room table. She would wake us up for school and for church. She would take us with her wherever and whenever she could. Helen, Sydney and little Zion. I came to believe that grandma was most proud of us. To her, we were actually reachable.

But as Sydney matured, she began to become more and more defiant. When grandma sent us off to school, she had no idea that I was the only one going. Sydney would skip school and hang out with the older kids.

Sydney eventually met a guy from South Philadelphia named Rameek. He was about nineteen years old, but had boyish charm that easily impressed Sydney. Sydney fell for Rameek. We would see Sydney less and less.

At fourteen, Sydney became pregnant. When grandma learned about her pregnancy and discovered her whereabouts, she was heartbroken. Instead of reacting angrily grandma became quiet. And Sydney ran away.

During her unplanned pregnancy, Sydney abandoned us all. She separated herself from her family and close friends and neglected to visit doctors. Throughout Sydney's pregnancy she smoked cigarettes and weed. And she had gained more than the recommended amount of weight.

We didn't even know Sydney's due date. The result of her decisions caused her to have an unhealthy pregnancy. Complications and pain forced Sydney to check herself into a hospital, where she learned it was time for her to give birth.

At the hospital, the doctors had to act quickly and coached young Sydney through the agonizing ordeal. It was only a few hours before my birthday, when we all learned that Sydney had given birth to a baby girl. She named her Rameisha. Sydney would now become middle school dropout and teenage mother. Her baby Rameisha was eager to prematurely enter this world. Rameisha came out feet first and almost died during labor: her spine was damaged, she couldn't move her arms or legs, and she relied totally on a ventilator because she could not breathe on her own.

Breech babies would typically be delivered by Caesarean section, but Sydney had not known the conditions of her baby during pregnancy. In fact this was the second time she had been in front of a doctor since she discovered she was pregnant. The intervening six months, Sydney intentionally and deliberately ignored the outside world. She assumed she could handle it on her own. She was wrong.

The man she chose to spend time with and distance herself from her family decided she was not important enough. Rameek left Sydney to fend for herself. The weight of being a teenage-single-parent left to raise an extremely sick paralyzed infant forced Sydney to abandon Rameisha. And the cycle of neglect continues. The abandoned mother, my sister, at fifteen withdrew from her daughter's life.

◆ ◆ ◆ ◆ ◆

TWENTY-FOUR
NOT SO SUDDEN SHOCK

When I was a child, I had terrible nightmares about losing my grandma. At first I couldn't bear the thought of grandma dying. After grandma's recent heart attack I began to accept it.

We all had our theories that grandma knew she was going to pass away soon. She was nicer and more giving. She talked with us more and told us stories.

She even said to me once before "I have to die."

"Don't say that!" I uttered in confusion.

No matter how tough I claimed to be, the thought of losing grandma weakened me. I would try to change the subject. I would attempt to get her to talk about more positive things.

"Did you see the new Law and Order episode?" I'd say. Or I would ask, "what's for dinner tonight?"

But no amount of denying or ignoring the inevitable would keep her with us. I wanted for us to focus on the here and now.

Even though grandma's health had made a downward spiral, she still continued to be active and productive. The school had to insist that she stay home from work. They encouraged her to retire and use her time to heal.

But at home grandma continued to be the rock of our family. She made sure she spent time with all of her grandchildren. She and I talked at length about my high school choices.

Actually, I began to feel proud of myself, particularly my renewed focus on writing. I talked with her about my goals of attending Carver high school. She knew how much of a better chance Carver High would provide me than my neighborhood high school. She was determined to see me succeed where my siblings had once failed. I believe my sister Sydney gave her the most trouble when she became a teenage mother. Grandma never talked with us about it, but we saw a change.

By now Zaire, America, and Sydney had all moved out of the house. Aunt Helena, her five children, India and I were still living with grandma. So the house was still full.

While the children were at school, grandma and Aunt Helena would stay home handling the needs of the family.

One Friday afternoon, I rushed home because I felt something was wrong. Unfortunately I was right. I walked into the house. Everyone was already emotional and in tears. My sister America rushed over to me and held me in her arms. She wept as she fought to say the words, "Grandma passed away."

I burst into tears. "No. No. No!" I cried. I felt lifeless. My heart sank to my belly. My body shook uncontrollably and the tears fell from my eyes. I was inconsolable.

Very quietly and peacefully on Friday May 29, 1998, Almighty God in his infinite wisdom gently closed the eyes of grandma and mercifully took her home to glory.

The reality was frightening to accept. In that moment I made a commitment to grandma that I would never forget her and that I would strive to make her proud.

My sister America stepped up the most after grandma died. She recognized how confusing my life would truly be. She recognized my dependency on grandma.

My mother and aunt Helena were struggling on their own and were equally traumatized by grandma's sudden departure. I don't recall ever talking about grandma's death with them. I remember my mother hugging me and consoling me and saying things like "I'm going to miss her so much" and "I know you miss her too." Yet, I don't recall her asking me how I felt. I don't recall her asking me what I would remember most about grandma.

◆ ◆ ◆ ◆ ◆

TWENTY-FIVE
GOODBYE GRANDMA

The day of grandma's funeral, I felt overwhelmed with emotions. Today will be the last time I get to see her in the physical form. But I promise, I will never forget her voice, her smell, and the way she treated me. My family had done their best to meet grandma's expectations. My aunt Helena and my mother discussed at length grandma's funeral and burial requests. Grandma had somehow articulated to my aunt the exact color pink she wanted to be buried in and decided on an ivory-color for her coffin. These matters were never explained to or discussed with us children, we weren't considered mature enough.

Zaire and I wore black tuxedos with a white flower pinned to our lapels. America, India, and Sydney wore beautiful black box dresses. Before the funeral, our older cousins and other family members stopped by the house to show their love and support to us. Even though Golden Gate Baptist Church is directly around the corner from our house, we rode in a black limousine.

Over two hundred people crowded into the small church to pay their respect. My grandma's obituary was pink like grandma's dress. It was the most creative obituary I had ever seen. On the cover was grandma's favorite picture from work. Because she worked at an elementary school, all staff members received complimentary photos from the photography company. Grandma always proudly displayed her photos in our home. Inside of the obituary were pictures of grandma's siblings, who had all passed away, and our current immediate family.

Her obituary was beautifully written. Grandma was born on January 21, 1937 in Lamar, West Virginia, to the late Creed and Annie Mae Copeland. She was the fifth child of that union. Like grandma, I am also the fifth child.

Although there were so many people present here to show their respects, I was surprised to learn that grandma's life was exceptionally limited to Philadelphia. It read that she received her formal education in the West Virginia Public School system. She graduated with honors in 1955. She later moved to Philadelphia. And the rest of life was spent in

Philadelphia. Grandma had gone to the Philadelphia School for Practical Nursing in 1962. She also went to Community College where she graduated from the school of sign language. And then grandma worked at Robert Morris Elementary School as a Lunchroom Aid and then as a program Assistant. That was her life.

Next it highlights her religious affiliations. It read that she joined Sanitary Methodist Church being a faithful member until they moved. She later rejoined the Golden Gate Baptist Church, there she remained until her death. To know Helen (or Major as she was affectionately called) was to love her.

Many people came to show their support. Scooter, Sam and Jamaal came. Ms. Sample, Mrs. Johnson, Mrs. McArthur, Mrs. Lewis, and Mr. El came. After viewing grandma's body, they each hugged me. It felt awesome to know that I was cared for and supported.

Grandma's passing saddened the entire family. She left to mourn two daughters; my mother Savannah and my aunt Helena, ten grandchildren; Zaire, America, India, Sydney, London, Lydia, Lateefah, Messiah, Mashaad, and me. Nevertheless, her funeral was full of love. Even though we many of us aren't mature enough to understand right now what losing a loved one means. We can feel in our hearts that grandma loved us.

The Golden Gate Baptist church choir sang "Blessed Assurance," one of grandma's favorite songs. The teachers from the elementary school where grandma worked also spoke. Mrs. Andrea Wilson-Harvey and Ms. Ruby Weaver, and the principal Mr. Gorodetzer all shared their testimony. Mr. Robert Miller sung "Mama" by Boyz II Men. The most touching part for me was my sister America's rendition of Phyllis Hyman's "Meet me on the Moon." I cried incessantly as she sang. It was difficult for me to hear Reverend Robert Walker as he gave grandma's eulogy.

Loss is hard. Grandma's passing happened without warning. But it has brought the family together in a meaningful way. Grandma's funeral was beautiful and I am sure she would be proud of her two daughters. Hopefully we continue to show this love.

◆ ◆ ◆ ◆ ◆

TWENTY-SIX
ACCEPTED

Scooter had already learned that he was accepted into Carver High. I unfortunately was not accepted. The administrative staff had received the notifications from the different high schools and notified parents by sending letters home.

The pain from grandma's death had already weighed heavily on my heart. It was even more painful to cope with being rejected from Carver High School. This was the most important thing to me right now.

But unbeknownst to me, I had a team praying for my success. What I did not know was that Mr. El, along with Mrs. Lewis and Mrs. Young had already discussed with my grandma their plan to get me accepted into Carver High School. This was just weeks before grandma had passed.

Mr. El visited the principal of Carver High School on my behalf. He wanted to get me into the high school. Although I had great grades and had been recognized for my writing, I was denied entry because of my below-average standardized test scores. What the test did not show was my grandma's conviction and a beautifully written letter she had wrote on my behalf.

Mrs. Travis, the principal of Carver High School at that time, had a fierce reputation and was known for having high academic standards for her school. Despite her reputation, Mr. El and Mrs. Lewis turned out to be two of my strongest allies. They went to the school with a letter my grandmother had written Mrs. Travis. In the letter, grandma had begged Mrs. Travis to consider me for admission into the magnet high school. It was extremely important for me to have this opportunity. My grandma asked her to listen to the Lord and to allow me entry into the high school.

Mrs. Travis agreed to think about it for a few days and Mr. El reminded her that graduation was only days away. The team of Vaux administrators succeeded in getting me an interview with Mrs. Travis herself.

Several days later, she asked Mr. El and I to come to her office. This time it was just Mr. El and I. I was so excited.

"I have decided to accept you as a student," she told me.

And although grandma is not here right now to witness my excitement, I know that she is smiling down on me. Although I really wish she had the opportunity to see how excited I am right now, I am ever grateful to know that people value her words and care about me.

This experience reminded me that maybe all of her work is not in vain. I am extremely grateful for educators like Mrs. Travis and Mr. El.

◆ ◆ ◆ ◆ ◆

To Love, from Zion

TWENTY-SEVEN
SWEE PEE

A few things in my life convinced me that being a thug or perpetrating to be hard is not the way for me. First recognizing the sacrifices my grandma made for me throughout my childhood, helped me to appreciate hard work. Now that grandma has passed away, I find it ever more important to succeed in life. As a black youth, my chances and opportunities are limited. As a fatherless child, I will probably have to learn many lessons the hard way. Similarly, as an abandoned child I'll probably have difficulties sustaining relationships.

Second, in my neighborhood young people who look like me die young. The news is saturated with stories of violence in Philadelphia. It seems summer time bring out the worst in everyone. I can speak from experience because in our neighborhood we've lost many young people.

Just recently we lost one of my favorite people, Swee Pee. Swee-Pee was my brother, Zaire's age. He and Zaire grew up together and were close friends. The poet in me appreciates people like Swee-Pee. So I write.

Swee-Pee was idolized on our north Philly corner
Fresh cut, clean clothes, he was a charmer
He stayed cool with the people, show love
Show he's equal, and so proud of
Being young gifted and black
So it was paper he'd chose to stack
He sold crack, shooting craps
Never aware that it's trap

So typical for a ghetto tale
Especially for a young black male
North Philly corners see you working on bricks
Swee-pee shooting craps Cee-lo 4 5 6
He'd say Zion got a head like a loaf of bread
Flat in the back can't fit no hat, then he said
Stay off these corners, stick to the book
Stay in school it's a much better look

North Philly saw how he was living

Noticed all the love he was getting

Swee-pee shooting craps Cee-lo 4 5 6

Head in the clouds, he's all up in the mix

never noticing he's taking a risk

Haters lurking, plotting ways to trick

Sweet in too deep taking all they money

Charming fellow pleasantly thinking its funny

Yet the allure of the game is a shame

Pulled Sweet right into its flame

Swee-pee shooting craps 4 5 6

Seven shots of lead hit him quick

At his home, someone caught him slipping

Now the whole neighborhood is tripping

Saying how angels don't die, no goodbye

It's see you later, pour a drink or get high

Now Mother's crying holding their crucifix

And we all on the corner holding candlesticks

Saying how much we will miss Swee-Pee

A young black male who inspired me

It's a shame he chose a loosing game

Young gifted black male soon became

A tragic tale of North Philly's streets

Swee-Pee, someone you'd be happy to meet.

Reflecting on Swee-Pee's death leads me to my third realization, appreciate life. Swee-Pee would never see his twenty-second birthday. The violence of these North Philadelphia streets has taken another life. This pattern of violence murders young men and destroy families. Swee-Pee's life simply added to another statistic. A number added to the city's murder rate. Swee-Pee would not be mentioned on the evening news. He was not a member of a church. And he won't have a fancy funeral. Just a normal funeral at a funeral home for another young black male, lost to the violence of the streets.

◆ ◆ ◆ ◆ ◆

TWENTY-EIGHT
PAIN

Suddenly I am beginning to realize that maybe the neglect I experienced growing up is actually a motivating force for me to become a strong and independent person. Being without and with less helped me to appreciate the little things. The time I spent without my mother and without my father helped me to appreciate the people I had in my life. Maybe the trauma from my childhood is a lesson on perseverance. Will I fail or will I succeed? I have been lucky to overcome my anger issues. And I'm grateful to the people who help me understand that me acting out was a result of my anger at my parents.

Around here, there are many young people who have experienced worse conditions than neglect. So when I see young people acting out, I can't help but think what happened to them to make them so angry. Not everyone my age is mature enough to understand. For instance one kid in my neighborhood he could not cope with his childhood trauma. I wrote about him before.

Pain doesn't always translate in conventional ways
From as far as I recall, Deon had an evil glint in his eyes
Like a devil, he mutilated dolls, broken bottles and windows
Everyone has a boiling point, but Deon was always boiling
He petrified little sisters and cousins
Petrified neighbors and pets

Pain doesn't always translate in conventional ways
Some days we'd find Deon crouched on all four legs
Between parked cars meowing for cats
Some days we'd find Deon throwing bottles at walls
Between abandoned homes or vacant lots
Some days we'd find Deon breaking pay phones for loose change

Pain doesn't always translate in conventional ways
Hurting others eased the feeling of abandonment
Abuse and neglect had trained him to be sadistic and mean
The truth hurts my heart to tell, Deon was touched once
By his mother's boyfriend

Made my heart understand

Pain doesn't always translate in conventional ways
Abuse never just hurts one person
And it probably didn't begin with the abuser
Trouble finds us all, Hurt children destroying things
Falling in love with power, Cycling through the trauma
Fragile little boy, tormenting cats and younger sisters
Future victims, creative struggle
There's always more to our stories
Pain doesn't always translate in conventional ways.

◆ ◆ ◆ ◆ ◆

To Love, from Zion

TWENTY-NINE

RAP DREAMS

Middle school changed me. I entered as a good boy. I entered as the boy who always wanted best friends and to know what it was like to be popular. I was used to being recognized for perfect attendance, for honor roll, and for having my writings published in the school paper.

The children in my neighborhood are cruel. So I had to learn how to be cruel as well. It took me a long time to build my team of real friends. Growing up on Newkirk Street in a not so pretty house won me a lot of ridicule. But these experiences proved to be revolutionary.

With grandma's passing, I became more and more independent. Relying less on my family, I found myself confiding more with my friends.

Growing up, I never found it difficult to make friends. I was always well liked and approachable. But when it came to having dependable friends who would protect you and fight for you, I only had two or three. My best friends are Jamaal, Sam, and Scooter.

At school my best friend is Scooter. Scooter was very influential in getting me interested in chess and I was excited because we both were going to Carver High School together.

Jamaal, Sam, and I were inseparable. Jamaal and Sam were both committed friends. We have been loyal to one another during our years as friends.

We hold each other accountable for our individual goals. Jamaal has always been very focused on accomplishing his goals of being a better rapper and writer. He makes me feel like a younger brother. He was extremely effective at getting things done.

We graduated from basketball dreams to rap dreams. We all had dreams of becoming successful rappers.

Growing up, you'd never see us apart. The Kirk boys were truly my heart. Best friends Sam Mueller Jay Steel. We really thought that we were for real. I guess it was circumstances of living poor in the hood. Deep down everyone knew we were good.

Summer summertime in Philadelphia is beautiful. The city of brotherly love is full of festivities, block parties, and cookouts. Jamaal, Sam, and I would hang out on the block.

We graduated from collecting snakes from snake hill, lemons from Fairmount Park, and stealing golf balls from the golf course. We all wanted to be famous rappers. So we stopped being child-like and we began idolizing our hood. Everyone knew deep down we were good.

Growing up on Newkirk Street, we listened to Gillie Da Kid, Dutch, Spade-O, and Major Figgas. You would find us touting our strength and reciting lyrics from Beanie Sigel, Freeway, State Property, to Eve the First Lady of Ruff Ryders. No matter how violent the lyrics we memorized them and emulated what we thought was necessary to fit into the era. Everyone knew deep down we were good.

Middle school changed me, not negatively. Clearly, I am evolving. I now have great friends. We found our sense of belonging with one another.

◆ ◆ ◆ ◆ ◆

THIRTY

TO LOVE, FROM ZION

Sometimes the noise at home becomes so overwhelming that I find it hard to think. There are too many people living here. It's too hard to relax and even harder to write.

The best remedy to a noisy house is to go outside. I'm going for a walk. Newkirk Street then a left on Thompson Street. I need to think. I need to hear my own voice.

As I approach 26th street, I walk past Robert Morris Elementary School. Memories of grandma fill my mind. This is not just where she worked. This is also my elementary school. Grandma walked us to school everyday. From the day I entered kindergarten here, grandma was consistent. Even as a fifth grader grandma made sure we walked to school together.

I turn left on 26th street and walk toward the Rec center. I think most clearly when I walk and I am able to hear my own voice.

My voice is important. My story must be told. I have had many reasons to be overwhelmed. This year alone, I lost grandma. In our neighborhood, we lost Swee-Pee and Damien. I've had many reasons to be cynical and angry. However these experiences have taught me to be more wise and conscientious. Most importantly I'm learning to find the love in all situations and circumstances.

I make it to the Rec center and it's the perfect night to sit at the park. I find an empty bench. Many teenagers come here. But tonight there are many available places for me to sit and reflect.

As I relax, I have much to reflect on. I'm excited about attending Carver High School. A new school and a fresh start is what I need in my life. I have no time to worry about mommy issues or consume myself in what-ifs about my father.

It's time to evolve. Things change. Times will get better. My main goal is to seek love. Search for the love. Through the pain I've learned to overcome the pain with love. Search to find the love in all things even the tumultuous and bizarre. For a while, the problems of life clouded my vision.

But now I have an opportunity to learn to see my goal with faithful eyes.

As I walked back home, this time I took Masters Street back home. This walk home reminds me of Vaux Middle School. I usually walk down Masters Street to get home. The familiar faces recognize me. I nod and wave to the people I know.

When I got home, the house was still noisy and all of my cousins were talking over television. My Aunt Helena had ordered Chinese take-out for everyone. "Zion, I got you a shrimp broccoli," she said.

I thought to myself, I love my Aunt Helena. She always makes sure I eat.

"Thank you," I said.

I smiled and accepted the platter. Aunt Helena was conscious of my emotions. However, she said nothing. I sat with my cousins and my aunt. Together we ate our Chinese take-out and they continued to talk about television.

◆ ◆ ◆ ◆ ◆

THIRTY-ONE
ANGELS ARE REAL

From my point of view, I have had many mother like figures in my life. Although Savannah Major gave birth to me, my mothers include my grandma, my aunt, my older sister America, and some of the teachers and administrators from my school. Often times, the older women in my life taught me more than I had learned from my own mother. Or by recognizing my material needs, they came through for me when I needed school supplies, clothes, or food to eat.

These women helped me to discover that angels are real. At several different junctures in my life, angels have rescued me. I believe that Grandma is an angel. Not only in life but also in her death she continues to watch over me.

Our spiritual and emotional connection can never dissipate. I continue to strive to make her proud. In many ways,

I still consider myself a young boy struggling to make sense of my complex life. I remember feeling abandoned and alone. She was never far to remind me how wrong I truly was.

I had father-like figures too even though these men shared no DNA with me. Mr. El was not only the chess coach but he was also a great administrator at our school. Seeing a strong black man everyday gave me hope that one day I could grow up to be a responsible career driven man. I believe that my mentor Mr. El is an angel.

I believe that my English teacher Ms. Annette Sample is an angel. And I believe that my mentor Mrs. Lewis is an angel. She taught me to put it all in god's hands. What an invaluable lesson to instill in a young man. And likewise, I believe that my mentor Mrs. Johnson is an angel. The Johnson family has taught me structure. To me they taught me that black families like the Cosbys are actually real. Both Mrs. Johnson and Mr. Johnson have taken an interest in my success, even inviting me to their home and to their church. Mother and father attending church instilling values in their children. I spent many holidays and family outings with the Johnson family.

Angels are real. When we acknowledge and show appreciation for our blessings, our angels are activated. We can grow with our angels as their power is intensified through prayer and acts of kindness.

Why prayer? Prayer is one of the most powerful tools in the world. Prayer is more than a spiritual experience; it has the power to change a person's conscience and subconscience. When we pray we make a spiritual connection with a greater power, often times we make praise or show gratitude for our blessings. I believe that prayer activates the positive energy needed for angels to thrive. The more you pray the more blessings will come to you.

❖ ❖ ❖ ❖ ❖

To Love, from Zion

THIRTY-TWO
POMP AND CIRCUMSTANCE

"How many tickets do you have?" I asked Scooter.

"I managed to get eight tickets," Scooter said.

"I got six."

It amazed us that we only received three tickets for our eighth grade commencement ceremony.

"Who only has three family members?" I asked sarcastically.

"Yeah." Scooter said.

"Right, like I already know that some families are going to storm into that church with or without a ticket."

"All my family coming," Scooter said. "Especially since Demetrius and I are both graduating."

"Well I hope they don't turn my peoples away," I said. "Not that they'll make it on time."

We call it graduation. They call it a commencement ceremony. I call it one of the best days of my short life.

Graduates arrived early so that we could be arranged by our last names and in position for the start of the ceremony. Families waited outside of the church until graduates were accounted for and in position. As expected, I knew some people would be late. I wasn't particularly concerned as long as everyone made it to see me walk down the aisle to "Pomp and Circumstance."

We heard the church organs begin to play. Then after the musical instruments and microphones were tested, the ceremony was set to begin.

"Let's go," I shouted out to my fellow graduates.

There was a collective sigh of relief. And several students could be heard yelling "yes," "it's about time," and "let's go."

"Pomp and circumstance" was played and the organizers scurried to prepare us students. As the music played we sauntered in a two-step fashion into the main sanctuary. Parents jumped to their feet and began applauding. Cameras flashed. Names were yelled unintelligibly. The march continued. When I saw my mother, my sister America, and my Aunt Helena, I waved and smiled. I put my hands back behind my back and continued to saunter the two-step march we practiced.

It was expected to hear parents shouting their child's name. It was their way of showing pride, even though it interrupted the flow of the ceremony. And all throughout the ceremony names were shouted out at random. I can't even recall a single speech because there was so much going on. Nevertheless, I am filled with emotions right now.

I wish grandma was here to see me. My face is puffy and eyes are full of tears. My nose is red from wiping away the accumulated snot. How is it that joy feels so similar to pain? It was only a few days ago I was crying similarly at grandma's funeral.

There are three reasons why this commencement ceremony is so important. First, it's amazing to bring family together for positive events. Thus far, I have put myself under a lot of pressure to not end up following the mistakes of others. No disrespect to my siblings, but I am grateful to be able to witness their setbacks and recognize that their path is not the path for me. This ceremony gives us an opportunity to heal emotional wounds. By celebrating a victory or accomplishment together, it is helping us to cope with the sorrow of grandma's death.

Which brings me to the second reason why this ceremony is so important, it would make my grandma proud. Unfortunately, I have been branded as "grandma's boy." I have earned this reputation because grandma has been the most active family member in my life. I regret not telling her "I love you" more often and for not showing her how grateful I was for her. So this ceremony is my way of making her proud.

Third, and perhaps the most important, this ceremony makes me proud. For I have imagine this day for a long time now. I have endured other people putting limits on my potential. Despite being fatherless and at most times without my mother, I have found a way to use those obstacles as an advantage. My story has made people pay attention to me. But I had to be courageous enough to share it.

◆ ◆ ◆ ◆ ◆

THIRTY-THREE
FOR MY PEOPLE

For my people, the conscious person, the thinker, the worker, the practitioner, the researcher, the learner, the student, the teacher, the lovers of the world. The ones who recognize the undeniable presence of community in our world. The ones who choose to participate. The ones who recognize the irrefutable need to build community.

For my people and their words, phrases, clauses, sentences, paragraphs, and their narratives. Their stories seldom told but we know they have one. Their voices never shared but we know they have one. The ones often silenced because of their race, culture, gender, or religion. Shut down and shut out by teachers, students, and family. Shut down by people who choose not to listen for their voice.

For my people who compete to make ends meet, try hard to do better, make every effort, fight, scramble, scuffle, tussle, wrestle, battle because it's your right. I see you. There is an upside to your bad. Your life is still in process. You are creating your present. We are creating our future.

For my people, political because we're a community, conscious cause it's our duty, yearning for unity craving for change, committed to find a way to make a better day. Remember we are not alone, that we need each other. We must learn from one another and value the power of education.

For my people, teachers, learners, not afraid to combat the inequities of mainstream policies. Lesson planning, organizing, researching, thinking critically and consciously about the many minds we are responsible for developing.

For my people, school students studying seriously. Eager for knowledge, yearning for unity craving for change. So often misguided, misunderstood, misinterpreted and misrepresented. The ones who rebel because they're dissatisfied with false-idols and failed guidance. Follow your own dreams. Reach for your own stars.

For my people khaki pants, green polo, backpacks, pen, and paper. Back to school. Brand new gear or hand-me-downs doesn't matter because they're here to learn. For my people who rise 6:30 in the morning to get to school by 7:30, for my people who walk miles, catch buses, ride the subway, and elevated trains to make it to school everyday.

For my people who don't seem to understand the beauty that lives within them. For my people who sometimes don't realize the beauty that they possess. For my people intelligent, brave, wise, resilient, we've seen a lot, but we want more.

For my people, who I believe in, despite the days, I feel discouraged, upset, frustrated, confused, this is for you, you are brilliant, you are wise, you are creative, you are unique. Lift your arms high. You will persevere. Follow your dreams, be true to yourself, love your world, this is for my people.

◆ ◆ ◆ ◆ ◆

To Love, from Zion

I AM FROM GRANDMA'S LOVE

I am from grandma's love, momma's neglect, and daddy's abandonment. Three sisters, one brother, house full of yelling, fighting for attention and no one's winning.

I am from her prayers that I live a full and abundant life. From a city where LOVE lives, not just in a park but also in classrooms and small churches that sit on corner blocks.

I am from North Philly, 29th and Thompson Street, neighborhood submerged in crack, weed, stray cats, broken bottles and empty vials like glitter on the concrete.

Our row home, house full of kids, aunts and cousins sharing everything, nothing of my own

I am from dysfunction. Loose cigarettes and packs of menthol Newport cigarettes, from addiction to drugs and alcohol, crack heads, blunt wraps and Dutch masters.

I am from a struggle. A gloomy home. Cooking on a hot plate. Pork-n-Beans hot dogs, Beef-a-roni, Ravioli, Oodles-n-Noodles, Papi Store, Chinese Store family struggling to get by.

I am from "Where's Mommy?" and "I wish Mommy was here." From reassuring hugs from a grandmother who cares. I am from crying cause Momma's gone and no where to be found. Crack caught her attention and left us to be found. Grateful for grandma's grace, thankful for her love

I am from Robert Morris Elementary School—right around the corner; wrestling with my friends, testing who was stronger; Slap boxing, Fistfights, toe-to-toe, proud cause you're the toughest. All the while hiding behind the pain that we're suffering

I am from School House Rock. I am from Sesame Street and playing school since the age of three. I'm from curb ball, hopscotch, O'clocks, and hide-n-seek; I'm from basketball at the Rec, rough house, horse, one-on-ones. I'm from freeze tag, 1-2-3 red light… and racing from corner-to-corner.

I am from Vaux Middle School. Gotta fight to show I'm tough. Gotta prove I aint no punk. Honor roll, smart guy, what's he tryna prove. Yes I'm smart but I'm not weak, daring to be tested. All the while hiding behind the pain that I am hurting.

I am from the smell of hot coffee and WDAS in the morning; listening to the sounds of gospel and smooth R&B. From "this is the day, this is the day, that the lord has made."

From leaving the corner behind. The block has no love for young black men like me. I'm from recognizing dead ends and roadblocks. I'm from discerning right from wrong.

I am from grandma raising her entire family. The 5'2, 110 pound giant. The queen of her throne doing her best to survive. And we survived.

I am from saying goodbye to grandma far too soon. I'm from never forgetting grandma, keeping her with me everywhere I go.

And now I can say that I am from George Washington Carver High School. Maybe this school will provide me with better opportunities. The opportunities grandma wanted me to have. The opportunities my teachers want me to have.

I am from hopes and prayers. Writing in a book cause there's no one to listen. Surrounded by people but feeling completely alone.

I am from humility. I am from learning to keep my mouth closed. I am from minding my own business.

I am from love, grandma's love, momma's neglect, and daddy's abandonment. We should seek out love, even in horrible situations. For this I have made my purpose. The quest for love fuels me. Where there is love there is God.

◆ ◆ ◆ ◆ ◆

To Love, from Zion

To Love,
From Zion

Journaling Activities

HARREAM PURDIE

Through journaling you can discover a lot about yourself. This section provides readers with writing ideas. When journaling, there are no rules—just write. Be open, be emotional, be honest, be silly, and write whatever you want.

Write to Cope with Neglect

- Write about a time when someone neglected you or forgot about you. How did it make you feel?

- Briefly describe a plight that you experienced as a young child. What was the outcome?

- Do you see great disparities of wealth in your community? Where do you see them? Who is being neglected?

- Have you ever turned a negative situation into a positive one? In what aspect of your life did this occur? Explain.

- Write about a time you held your tears.

- Finish the following sentences:
    o I am afraid that . . .
    o I'd forgive him/her but . . .

- Reflect on a time you felt anger/rage.
- Finish the following sentences:
    o What really makes me angry is . . .

Identity and Finding Oneself

- Think of an important event or incident in your life. What lesson did you learn from it? Write a well-developed personal narrative that describes the experience and reveals why it was important to you.

- What is the story behind your name? What does your first name mean? What is the origin of your name, (where does it come from)? Do you know where your last name comes from? Write about what your name means to you and how you got your name. If you love your name, describe how that makes you feel? If you dislike your name, describe why and what you would change your name to if you could.

- Create your own "Where I'm From" poem, by listing the sights, sounds, smells, tastes, and feelings associated with your childhood, family, and life experiences.

- Create your own "I am" poem. be sure to include special characteristics, something you love, something you desire, and imaginary sights and sounds.

Writing about Goals

- I am happiest when . . . .

- My dream for my future is . . .

- When I was growing up, I always thought I would be . . .

- Since then, my goal has been to become . . .

- The colleges that I am considering are . . .

- My dream career would be . . .

- In order to reach my goals and dreams, I need to . . .

- It's always been a dream of mine to travel to . . .

Writing about Love

- What are five things you love? Extend your understanding by elaborating on why you love those five things.

- Name five people you love. What qualities do they possess individually?

- Have you ever experienced unrequited love? How did it make you feel to know or to learn that the love was not returned?

- How do you celebrate your loved ones? Do you like to give them gifts? Do you express how you feel about them? Do you write personalized letters?

- Make a recipe for love. What is required to make someone feel loved? What are some ways people express their love for another?

Reflecting on People and Memories

- The lyrics of a popular song suggest that people do not realize what they have until it is gone. In a narrative essay, write about an aspect of your past that you appreciate now more than ever.

- Think of a moment from your middle-school years in which you realized that you had a specific strength or talent. In a well-written personal narrative, retell the events of that episode. Use dialogue and sensory details to make the experience come alive for readers.

- Tell the story of a dream or use images from a dream you can remember.

- Write about a memory, but pretend it happened to someone else.

- When was the last time you had to compromise? What was the situation and were you happy with the results?

- Name a recent endeavor of yours that ended in success and one that ended in failure.

Writing about Literacy

- In your own words, define **literacy**. Based on your own definition, what is your earliest recollection of literacy?

- Do you remember learning to read? Describe the learning experience. How did it make you feel to succeed at learning to read?

- Why is it that children love to read but dislike reading to learn for school?

- What are the qualities of a good reader? What are the qualities of a good writer?

- Where was your favorite place to go as a child? Why?

- Tell about your favorite childhood book and explain what you like about it.

To Love, from Zion

ACKNOWLEDGMENTS

This book would not have been possible without Annette Sample. Thank you for helping me to develop into a better writer. You have been more than a teacher to me. You have been a mentor and a mother to me. It was in your classroom that I discovered social justice and the power of writing. Your assignments broadened my perspectives and taught me how to plan my own life. Thank you for embracing my vision with your heart and for your commitment, which is evident in all that you have done.

I want to also thank Joseph J. Pye, my cousin. Your attention to detail is unrivaled. No matter the distance, our friendship has remained the same. I value your perspective and your insight. You've always been there for me sharing life experiences and wisdom. We have equally strengthened one another and for that I am immensely grateful.

I would like to thank my good friends Ericka Williams and Zuri Monae for helping me out during a time of need. You were both there for me to listen to my stories and encourage me. Ericka, whether you realize it or not, I am a better person because of our friendship. Zuri, you inspire me to produce art and to allow art to speak for itself. Thank you both for affirming my writing and me.

To my nieces and nephews, each story in this book is meant to build you up. I hope these stories encourage you to remember yourself and to follow your own dreams. Thank you for reading.

To my students, I hope this book is a call to writing. I intend this book to be a brief framework for story telling. Although the poems, reflections, and vignettes are from my personal experiences, many came to life in the classroom. I encourage you to write your stories.

To my mother, Stephanie Major. I love you unconditionally. The stories in this book reflect our past and my memories of my childhood. We have persevered through troubling times and I am blessed to have you. Thank you for life and for love.

To my family, friends, colleagues, and mentors, your prayers are always felt. Thank you for supporting and encouraging me to stay true to my nature.

◆ ◆ ◆ ◆ ◆

ABOUT THE AUTHOR

Harream Samaj Purdie was born and raised in Philadelphia and attended public schools. He is a writer, educator, and activist. He holds a bachelor's degree in English from Morehouse College and two master's degrees from the University of Massachusetts Amherst and St. Joseph's University. When he's not teaching and writing, he is most likely running or practicing photography. You can visit him at www.harreampurdie.wordpress.com.

◆ ◆ ◆ ◆ ◆

To Love, from Zion